a collection of short stories written by PONY magazine contributors

edited by Julia Goodwin
a PONY Magazine publication
DJ Murphy (Publishers) Ltd

First published in Great Britain by
DJ Murphy (Publishers) Ltd 1988

PONY Magazine
DJ Murphy (Publishers) Ltd
296 Ewell Road,
Surbiton,
Surrey KT6 7AQ.

Cataloguing in Publication Data

P tales.
Roman 1 Goodwin, Julia
823: 914[J]

ISBN 0 9513707 0 7

Designed by
Mark Gibbs
Assistant Editor
Diana Wallace
Typeset by Graphac,
181/191 Garth Road,
Morden,
Surrey SM4 4LL

Printed in the UK by
Hollen Street Press,
Slough,
Berks.

Contents

illustration by Claire Colvin

A LITTLE GREY FOAL

By Christine Pullein-Thompson

When Sharon's local riding school closes down there is nothing for her to do except babysit for other families on the estate. But her dreams come true when the Lamberts offer her the use of their paddock. Now all she has to do is buy a pony.

From the moment Littlecote Riding School closed down, I had wanted a pony. For two years I had helped there at weekends and in the holidays. I had saved every penny for riding lessons and second-hand riding clothes. Then suddenly, without warning, the whole establishment was sold to a developer for a million pounds.

I was eleven then and whenever another advertisement appeared offering desirable homes for thousands and thousands of pounds on the Littlecote estate, I felt like tearing it down. But the worst part was not knowing where the ponies went, because we were never told.

I lived with my parents and two brothers in Number Nine Derby Road, in a terrace house with a garden eighty foot long, three bedrooms and a lounge-diner. Both my parents were out at work, so were my brothers. I was the baby of the family and hated it.

Without the riding school I had nowhere to go and nothing to do at weekends except deliver the Sunday papers for Mr Crossman at the corner shop, and babysit for the Lamberts, who lived in a modern house and owned a paddock, which lay between them and the other houses on the estate.

Their baby was teething one evening and they were grateful because I managed to soothe him to sleep, so grateful that Mr Lambert said, "I've just thought of something Sharon. I know you want a pony. You can keep him in our paddock if you like. We won't charge you anything dear. You can have it for nothing."

"You don't mean it, not really?" I gasped. "Oh thank you." So now I started saving again. Every penny I earned went in a tin with *pony* written on its lid. Mum put spare change in it from time to time and once, when she was feeling rich, a five pound note. But Dad was against the whole idea.

"You haven't got the time and you'll never have the money," he told me. "Horses are for the rich Sharon, not for us."

"Oh yeah, you wait and see Dad," I replied.

Everybody seemed to want me for babysitting that long hot summer; by October I had over one hundred pounds in my tin. I knew that it wouldn't buy much, but I decided to go to the monthly horse sale in the cattle market just once, because that would give me an idea of how much money I needed.

It was held on a Friday and luckily it was half-term. I borrowed a money belt from one of my brothers and put my money in it. I was too excited to eat any breakfast. I had persuaded Richard, my best friend, to accompany me. He's tall, fair-haired and good at passing exams. We caught a bus together.

"I think you're crazy Sharon. What are you going to do with a horse?" he asked, paying both our fares.

"Ride it of course," I said.

The market was crowded with people and there were horses everywhere – thin, broken down, overweight; neighing wildly, looking for lost friends. Frightened, anxious, resigned. And a few, which I supposed had never been ill-treated or sold before, were looking interested and alert. I wiped my eyes with a tissue.

"You're not crying, are you?" demanded Richard.

"Yeah. What does it look like?" I retorted.

We watched them being sold in the big building beyond the pens. They went for hundreds of pounds, or most of them did.

"It's hopeless, they're too expensive. We might as well go home Sharon," Richard said, pulling at my arm.

"Not yet. Let's wait a little longer."

The sale was nearly over when a foal appeared, looking anxiously around for its mother. It brought a lump to my throat. It was mousey grey with a well-bred head, small, neat grey hoofs and a tail the shape of a fox's brush.

People were drifting away. Richard was still pulling at my arms when I raised my hand and called, "Fifty". And heard the auctioneer reply, "Fifty I'm bid, fifty."

"He's too small for you Sharon," Richard whispered.

"I don't care, I've got to save him," I whispered.

At first a tall, thin woman with a worn face was bidding against me, but at sixty pounds she dropped out and a fat man took over. I kept marvelling that I was being taken seriously, that no one had demanded to see my money first, or asked whether I was eighteen.

"One hundred," I shouted, raised my hand, my stomach churning.

"One hundred, I'm bid one hundred, for the last time one

hundred," shouted the auctioneer as his hammer fell.

"He's yours," said Richard, as though I hadn't noticed!

He was put in a pen with another foal. He had baby teeth and wouldn't eat the bread I offered him. Richard went with me to the auctioneer's office, where I handed over one hundred pounds, some of it in fifty pence pieces.

Then I said to the clerk, "I don't know how to get him home, that's the problem," while Richard sighed beside me.

"Ask the bloke over there," said the clerk, pointing at an enormous man with a hat on the back of his head, smoking a cigar. "He's called Mr Collins. He'll help you."

"Will do," Mr Collins said when I explained my predicament. "I'll deliver him, but it won't be 'til late afternoon. What's your address?"

Richard told him.

"Let's say four o'clock then. It'll cost you a fiver. And that's a lot less than I usually charge," Mr Collins said, smiling at us both.

Richard produced a fiver and gave it to him.

"You didn't have to," I said as we walked away. "But thanks all the same. I'll pay you back, I promise."

I said goodbye to Richard when we got off the bus. Then I rushed home and took the plastic bucket from under the sink and, filling it with water, carried it to the Lambert's field. After that I knocked on their back door, but they weren't at home and nor were Mum and Dad. Suddenly I felt alone and rather scared. What if I can't manage the foal? I thought. What if the Lamberts are angry? Supposing he leans over the wire and eats their roses?

A huge cattle truck was drawing up outside our house. A minute later Mr Collins was letting down the ramp and asking, "Where do you want him then?"

We took the foal to the field together, me pulling, Mr Collins pushing. "Bit small for you, isn't he?" he asked as I slammed the gate shut.

"Yeah. I'm not going to ride him. I'm going to look after him," I said.

"Well, I'll be off then," said Mr Collins, handing me a tatty hemp halter. "Best of luck."

I called the foal Prince because I wanted him to feel he was someone special. He spent that first evening walking round and round the small field, looking lost and frightened, and I knew he wanted his mother. Later, while it was still light, Mum, Dad and the Lamberts looked at him. Mum said he was a sweetie, Dad that he would be a lot of trouble. Prince kept his distance, trusting no one.

"Don't look so worried. He'll be alright with time, dear," said Mr Lambert, rumpling my hair.

"You can teach our kiddies to ride on him," suggested Mrs Lambert smiling.

"He's too young. He's just a little grey foal," I said.

I visited Prince every day. I brought him oats and bran from the pet shop. Soon he stopped looking for his mother, and looked for me instead. He would stand with his little head over the fence, and his nostrils would tremble as he saw me approaching along the road with his food. He knew the times of my visits exactly. The Lamberts fed him too, on apple peelings and bits of carrot.

Slowly October became November and the weather grew cold. I longed to buy Prince a rug then, but I hadn't enough money. I started to buy him bales of hay, pushing them home from the pet shop in a wheelbarrow. Soon rain fell in bucketfuls and I wished I could afford a shelter, but of course I hadn't enough money for that either. There were muddy patches in the field now, and busy moles threw up great mounds of dark earth. I seemed to be always in a mackintosh and muddy boots. Mum said that the house was beginning to look like a farmyard. The kitchen floor became muddy and my bedroom had bits of hay scattered everywhere.

I boiled up potato peelings for Prince and begged carrot peelings and cabbage leaves from my friends. I spent ages just talking to him, telling him that next year he would have a shelter and a brand new waterproof rug. For my birthday I asked for money, nothing else. There wasn't much babysitting available now and I needed every penny I could earn for hay.

I stopped seeing Richard when he told me I was beginning to look like a horse. I didn't miss him, because Prince was taking up all my spare time.

Soon Prince grew a thick coat. Frosts arrived and ice covered the two water buckets I had bought. Prince was always hungry. There was almost nothing left for him to eat in the field now; not a nettle, and hardly a blade of grass. As the days grew shorter I had less and less time to spend with Prince. On weekdays it was still dark in the mornings when I fed him, and dark when I returned from school in the evenings. Soon my torch battery ran out and I hadn't the money to buy another one. Then Richard dropped in one evening.

"Diane's having a disco at her place on Friday night. How about coming? It doesn't start 'til seven, so it won't affect your pony watching," he said with a laugh.

"Go on, go. You haven't been anywhere for ages," Mum said.

"But I haven't anything to wear and look at my hair!" I wailed.

"It doesn't matter. Jeans will do," Richard said. "You must go out sometimes."

I fed Prince quickly that evening. Then I washed my hair and had a bath. Mum lent me a blouse and I put on my best jeans and some high-heeled boots, which were too small and pinched my toes. Dad took me to the disco in the car. "Don't be late, do you hear Sharon? Be back by ten love. Ring up when you're ready to leave."

"Ten! Don't be daft Dad. Midnight's more likely," I cried.

It was lovely to be with my friends again. The music was deafening. And straight away Richard seized me by the arm crying, "Come on you pony girl, have a drink."

"I must be home by midnight. Dad will kill me if I'm not," I said.

"You will be. Don't look so worried Sharon," said Richard laughing.

After a time everyone seemed to be a long way off, rather as though I was looking down binoculars the wrong way round. Then I started to feel giddy.

"She had better lie down for a bit," Diane said. She sounded hazy and miles away, and everything was going round and round. I lay on a divan and someone put a blanket over me. And I kept thinking of Prince, waiting for me. Several times Diane leaned over me to ask, "Are you alright? Are you sure?" And all I could do was smile in return. Then everyone was gone. Someone had left a side light on, and there was a faint glow from the street lamp outside.

Diane appeared again. "Are you alright? We've spoken to your Dad.

My Mum will run you home first thing, alright?"

I nodded. My head was still spinning and I felt very tired.

When I woke again it was morning. My mouth was dry and my head felt on fire. I sat up and started shouting straight away, "What about Prince? I haven't fed Prince. He'll be starving."

"Stop yelling, you'll wake everyone up," said Diane appearing in a dressing gown. "Calm down. Why did you buy him anyway?"

"Because he needed a home. I've got to go home at once," I cried looking for my boots. "What's the time?"

"Eleven o'clock."

Eleven o'clock! And rain was cascading down outside.

"Mum will take you," Diane said. "Mum, where are you Mum?"" Her mother was young and beautiful.

"Don't you want any breakfast?" she asked.

I shook my head. "I've got to feed Prince," I said.

"Prince is her pony," explained Diane, sounding exasperated.

A few minutes later I was on my way home, the windscreen wipers working full speed. "Can't your parents feed the damned pony?" Diane's mother asked.

"No, they don't know anything about ponies," I said. "Anyway, Mum and Dad are not like that, they're not that sort of parents; they're always working, if you know what I mean. And anyway I didn't ask them. I said I would be home by midnight."

There was a horsebox parked by the field gate and a small crowd of people. My stomach was knotted as I leapt out of the car shouting, "Thanks awfully". Then I was running towards the field, my heart hammering. Next, I saw a police car and broke into a walk. Mum and Dad were there too. "There she is, there's Sharon," Mum shouted.

"We're taking your foal to the horse sanctuary," said a tall, thin woman with a worn face. "He needs a vet, a warm stable, and nursing."

"He got caught in the wire. Some girls on horses went by and he got caught up," Mum explained. "The girls rang the police."

But I knew what had happened. Prince had waited and waited for me to feed him and I hadn't shown up. I had let him down and now he was hurt and it was my fault.

"It's the best thing love," the policeman said. "We were going to call the RSPCA, but it's better if he goes to the sanctuary."

"But he's mine," I said in a small voice.

Prince was in the horsebox now, one foreleg scarlet with blood. He looked very small and alone.

"It's for the best Sharon," insisted Mum.

"I want him back, when can I have him back?" I asked shivering in the rain.

"You can come and visit him whenever you like. He's still yours. We're only a bus ride away. We always need people like you," said the lady from the sanctuary who was called Melanie Jones, throwing up the horsebox ramp. "It was no life for him here, was it? All alone. He's only a baby. He needs friends, he needs his hoofs trimmed and he needs worming. But he's still yours," she insisted, handing me a tissue. "We aren't stealing him."

"Can I see him tomorrow?" I asked.

"Of course, whenever you like. I saw you at the sale. We were bidding against each other for a time. I'll buy him from you if you like," she continued. "You saved him from the meat man Sharon and that's something."

I watched the horsebox leave. "You could have fed Prince," I said turning to my parents. "Just once."

"Once, twice, all the time, that's the way it goes. You couldn't cope, you know you couldn't. And the Lamberts are selling up; they're selling the field for building. I didn't tell you, because I knew you'd be upset, but now I can." Mum had her arm round my shoulder.

We were wet to the skin. The police and the horsebox had gone.

I looked at the field and saw it was a muddy little prison, where a small foal had stood all alone waiting for me, because there was no one else. I saw heaps of dung which had grown and grown.

Prince would have friends now. His hoofs would be trimmed. He wouldn't stand alone in the rain ever again, waiting by the gate for me to return from school.

"It's all for the best love," Mum said, opening our back door. "You just sit down and have a cuppa. You look terrible. Did you drink too much at the party?"

"I don't know. I passed out, and when I woke up, it was morning," I said. "I shouldn't have gone. I should have stayed and looked after Prince. I thought I would be home by midnight, I thought. . ." but really I didn't know what I thought any more.

"But I want him to stay mine," I said, slowly blowing my nose.

"You heard what the lady said. We'll all go there tomorrow. Dad will take us, won't you Dad?" asked Mum.

Dad was checking the football results. He looked up and nodded. "It's alright with me," he said.

So the next day the three of us went. Prince was with another foal in a loosebox bedded deep in straw. His leg was bandaged. He looked at me and nickered softly, and that seemed the nicest thing which had happened to me for a long time. Soon Melanie Jones appeared. "I'm so glad you saved him Sharon. I was desperate when we couldn't have him. Sadly we have limited funds," she said.

I knelt in the straw and Prince put his head on my shoulder and blew down my neck. And I knew that now he had all the things I could never have given him, which I had wanted him to have so much. "I'll come every weekend and help, if that's alright," I offered.

"That'll be lovely," replied Melanie Jones smiling.

"I'll have one of your collecting boxes too," I added.

We had arrived late and now it was time to leave. "See you next Saturday then," I said, getting into the car.

And now a great weight seemed lifted from my shoulders. The struggle for money and spare time for Prince had gone. He wouldn't be waiting in the muddy field for me any more. But I could still see him every weekend and in the holidays. And he would be alright now, whatever happened to me.

"Thank God, that's over," Mum said. "What you would have done without a field I don't know. Don't go buying another pony 'til you've got a good job and somewhere decent for him, please Sharon."

"I shall make my fortune or marry a farmer," I answered. I imagined an old farmhouse, acres and acres of land and Prince grazing in the midst of his friends, mine again and safe for ever.

★ ★ ★

illustration by Steve Humfress

THE TREASURE SEEKER

By Antoinette Lee

When Anna got locked in Herbie's stable one night, metal-detecting Martin came to the rescue. He was there again when she needed help to get her frightened pony through a tunnel of traffic. Trouble was, he was a trespasser...

The sparrow darted in and out among the rafters, snatching at the pony's feed. The thick, rich smell of wet straw and the steam rising from Herbie's back through the blue string sweat rug gave Anna a sense of homecoming.

No matter that the weather had been foul all day, her jacket and jodhpurs soaked, and Dad had said he couldn't collect her until seven. She had biscuits in her pocket to nibble if she felt hungry, and a full hour to complete the chores she usually rushed.

Autumn evenings. The lights were switched on in the stables and the familiar rustle of ponies and cross-talk of gymkhanas past and shows to come gave Anna a feeling of comradeship that she lacked at home and school. Tonight she was the last to leave.

At the stables she didn't have to think about exams looming up. The ponies with their velvety noses and warm, broad flanks gave her uncomplicated friendship. She'd always been mad on riding, and half a horse was better than no horse at all. It didn't really matter that she didn't own the sturdy fourteen-hand gelding she was settling down for the night.

She leaned against Herbie's rump to push him to the further side of the stall so she could get at the tack box and heard the high, arrogant voice of Miss Bickley floating in from the yard.

"I'll not have them on my land, do you hear?

"They're a menace, frightening the ponies, turning up along the hedgerow – not to mention digging up the lane when they think they've found something with those infernal machines. I suppose we can't keep them off the public footpath, tho' I've a good mind to plough it up."

Anna was a bit in awe of the woman who ran the livery stables. She was competent and high-handed with those who worked for her. Even Fowler, who never said anything to the riders, just glared at them from under his dark eyebrows, and then sullenly, rudely almost, went off to complete the jobs Miss Bickley assigned him.

"That wouldn't stop 'em," she heard him say. "They'll only be on at you to reinstate them. Besides, you wouldn't get the horses through. The lane would be waterlogged in this weather. You could threaten them with prosecution."

"Or shoot 'em!" Miss Bickley retorted.

Everyone knew Miss Bickley resented trespassers on her land, the few acres of grazing that hadn't been swallowed up by road improvements. An 'M' road had been started three years ago, almost cutting her off from civilization. She had fought courageously for the fields that remained – she'd gone to law about it – and she was determined they should not be built over.

She'd been featured in the local paper. That's when they learned her father's family had owned land there for hundreds of years. He'd been killed in the war and she'd built up the livery stables 'when the money ran out,' people said.

"Aw come now," she heard Mr. Fowler's harsh laugh. "You can't take the law into your own hands, ma'am. Metal detecting is only a hobby. They'll lose interest one of these days."

Anna heard them moving about the building and suddenly the main light snapped out.

"Damn kids!" she heard Miss Bickley say. Whether she was annoyed at finding the lights still on in what she assumed to be an empty stable, or she was still fuming over the boys out in the fields with their 'infernal machines', Anna couldn't tell.

She was uncomfortably aware of how black it was, and that it was unlikely that anyone else would come in. She would have to lock up the tack box and *feel* her way out.

Herbie seemed quite oblivious to her groping about beside him. His tail swished close to her face and she could hear him munching hay. Strange how much louder noises seemed in the dark.

She turned the huge key in the old box her father had given her for her tack and hoped she had remembered to put everything away. Curry comb, brush, rag, the tin of linseed oil. She didn't want Herbie to tread on anything. She rammed the key into her jodhpur pocket and opened and closed the loosebox bolt carefully. It was stiff and pinched her finger.

She blew Herbie a kiss and followed the rivulet of standing water in the drain to the barn entrance. The double doors were latched from the outside. She was shut in.

Anna began to panic. He father was due to collect her in a few minutes but she usually waited for him on the grass verge at the entrance to the stables. If she wasn't there he might assume she had accepted a lift from one of the other riders. He would be annoyed but not anxious.

She peered through the slit between the upper and lower doors. The timber-boarded buildings were black and menacing. She'd not noticed the bubbles of old tar on them before. The ponies in the first stalls breathed down their noses. Tentatively she called out, "Hi!"

There was no reply.

Usually Miss Bickley stayed some time in the tack room, but tonight the door was closed firmly. The farmhouse was fifty yards away. Anna would have to shout pretty loudly to make herself heard, and if Miss B was watching TV . . .

But someone had heard her. A gruff voice, quite near, said: "Alright. I'll come quietly."

Anna saw a boy of about her own age move out of the shadows. He was dressed in jeans and an anorak. She peered out at him.

"Don't be an idiot. This isn't a Western. Let me out, can't you?"

He looked surprised. Foolishly she waited while he fumbled with the latch. Together, they drew the doors close again.

"Lucky you were still here. Miss B locked me in. Accidentally," she added quickly, noting his expression. "Where do you keep your pony?"

"I don't," he said hurriedly. "Look, let's scarper. I'm not supposed to be here. I heard that horsy woman coming across the yard and made myself scarce. That man with her is carrying a shotgun."

Anna laughed. "She can be quite fierce, but I don't think she'd order him to use it. What are you doing, then? Trespassing?"

A car engine was running beyond the gate and Anna flung herself forward.

"Dad's here. Do you want a lift?" but the boy had gone.

Anna and Herbie almost tripped over him the following morning. She had ridden over the ridge, and down to the bottom of Long Meadow, into the field with hummocks in it. Drawing in from a canter, she felt Herbie stiffen and if she hadn't collected him, he would have shied. The boy was crouched down beside the hedge, and stood up as she crashed to a halt.

She was aware of a high-pitched bleep. Herbie had heard it before she did; that was probably why his ears were twitching. She stared at the machine, like a small vacuum cleaner, lying in the grass.

The boy flicked a switch and the noise stopped. Anna was off-balance and had to brace her legs to avoid tipping over Herbie's head.

"You . . . idiot!" she said furiously. "You'll be for the high jump if Miss B catches you. You could have brought us both down."

Curiosity overcame her. "What are you looking for, anyway? This is private property. Farmland. You won't find gold coins or anything here."

"Don't be too sure," he said, grinning. He picked up a rusty lump of metal. "Know what this is?"

She shook her head. "It looks pretty useless to me."

"Part of a billhook," I think.

She wasn't interested.

"Where did you get to last night?" she asked casually.

"I'd left my bike behind a hedge."

"Secretive sort of person, aren't you? Flitting about like that. Turning up here again like a bad penny." She laughed. "I can't see the fun in wandering about with a gadget like that."

"You'd be surprised what I turn up." Herbie, greedy as ever, was nuzzling at the boy's canvas bag.

"Nothing valuable. Just interesting. Buckles, D rings . . ."

"But why here? This has been fields for years."

"I happen to know," he said pompously, "this field was once a village. I'm looking for the midden."

"The what?"

"The rubbish dump".

"In the middle of nowhere?"

"Nowhere?" He looked across at the acres of new roadworks pierced by tunnels, connected by flyovers. "This is one of the busiest roads in England, always has been."

"Defacing the countryside. Putting traffic before people." She leaned over and patted Herbie's neck. "And horses."

"There's always been traffic here – horse traffic mostly. They've always been building roads and re-building them. Take this track here –"

"Bridlepath," Anna corrected him. "*No motorised vehicle*. That excludes you."

"Bridlepath, my foot! This was one of the main highways through the village. Straight as the crow flies to St Dunstans. Possibly Roman."

All the time he'd been speaking he'd been crouched again, picking away at a patch of exposed earth, his head turned away from her.

"There! What did I tell you?" He held up a horseshoe, worn thin and horribly rusty, but unmistakeable.

"Nothing to prove it's all that old. Could have dropped off one of the ponies . . ."

"I know where to find out. Hey, where are you going?"

"Just completing the circuit. We're jumping at a show this afternoon. I do it twice in the mornings."

"What about the woods over there. They look more fun. A bit limited isn't it? Riding round the same fields all the time?"

Anna wasn't going to admit why she didn't like going further afield.

"You'd better not be seen here again, know-all –"

"Martin, actually." He stood up. "Here," he said, handing her the piece of rusty metal. "You take it. Might bring you luck."

Just after lunch a pony came back lame, a jagged gash on its off hindleg. The rider, a small girl, was crying, and there was a burst of activity in the yard. Parents were sent for and the vet arrived. There was a smell of disinfectant, and everyone was tense and unhappy.

Miss B was rampaging about asking questions.

"Anyone seen an intruder? One of those boys with a metal detector?"

Anna could have kicked herself for being so friendly. She'd even tacked the worn shoe above Herbie's door and wondered if anyone had noticed it before she wrenched it off again. She felt sick and guilty, but hesitated before going directly to Miss B. She only knew Martin's first name and when she'd seem him, he was miles from where the accident had taken place. Unless he'd been working over the land for days, weeks even, he would never have got there.

Besides, she had to give him the benefit of the doubt.

She didn't know why she should. She put the shoe carefully in the tack box. Not that it was safe there. Ever since last night she'd been unable to find the key. She couldn't think what had happened to it. It was too big to overlook. Fortunately she hadn't locked the box properly. It wasn't the kind that clicked shut automatically, and it must have failed to 'catch.' At least she could get at the tack, but she was afraid it might be stolen.

They were always being warned about theft. Everything had to be marked with the owner's name. Even the ponies had been freeze-marked recently. A sudden thought made her feel worse. What if Martin . . .?

To reach the farm where the show jumping was to be held, she and Herbie would have to negotiate the spaghetti junction of new roads. Anna had been dreading it all week. At the last moment Tamsin had dropped out and she was going to have to take Herbie there alone.

Not that it was any different from other stretches of the motorway. The earth had been shifted, humped up, cut out, distorted. The cars whanged past every few seconds. Herbie plodded on.

It was the tunnel he didn't like. It was as if he tensed up the moment the concrete walls closed over him. The yellow lights high up cast an eerie, shadowless gloom. No footpath for pedestrians – or horses. She hugged the barrier and pressed with her heels to encourage him forward. Only one car passed them as they went through. Herbie moved faster as the natural daylight took over. They were through the first.

The second tunnel presented another obstacle. A huge yellow digger was parked to the left of the entrance, and a black plastic rubbish bag had been thrown over the seat. It flapped and fluttered like a large dead bird.

Anna just knew Herbie was going to make a fuss and tensed up in sympathy. That was fatal. Cars thrust past unheeding. Herbie balked. The tunnel was bad enough. The digger and flapping plastic were too much for even a reliable pony to take.

Anna tried everything. He threw up his head, danced sideways, backed out onto the road. She was almost in tears.

"Anything wrong?"

It was Martin. Cool and supercilious as ever, he slipped sideways down the embankment.

Anna was hot and sweaty already. Herbie, too, had begun to sweat; damp rivulets appearing in the glossy hair of his withers.

"Stupid idiots! Parking that monster just there."

"Out of the wind. Handy for Monday morning. You've got to see it from their point of view."

"Look! If I get off and lead him through, could you slow the traffic down or something? I'm scared he'll back out into a car."

"You're scared?" Martin echoed. She pretended not to hear.

"And you could get that plastic off."

Almost nonchalantly, Martin strode up to the machine and tore the plastic away, stuffing it into his pocket. Then he stepped out into the road and flagged the nearside lane of traffic to a halt. Anna scrambled off, walked to Herbie's head and stroked his nose.

"It's OK, honestly," she whispered, soothing him. He put his ears back and looked mulish.

"Oh come on!" she said, exasperated, trying to keep her voice from wobbling. Very gently, keeping herself between him and the digger, she led him forward.

Traffic on the opposite lane still whooshed past, making no attempt to slow down. But nothing overtook her as she stepped into the tunnel. Once past the 'yellow devil' he calmed down a little, almost trotting out of the other side. Swiftly, she led him up onto the verge and waited until the build-up of cars had streamed through.

Martin strolled out a few moments later.

"I thought you might have gone on," he said.

"Well, I had to thank you, didn't I?"

"Polite lot, aren't you, you horsy people? Threaten to shoot or prosecute one moment, the next being all haughty and gracious."

"Do I seem like that?" Anna was surprised. "I was scared, actually," she said. "My fear probably transferred itself to Herbie."

"So was I," he admitted cheerfully. "I felt such a fool just standing there. What if they hadn't slowed down? Perhaps they thought there'd been an accident."

"There could have been," Anna said grimly. "That beastly digger."

"You've got it in for those road engineers, haven't you?"

"Just look at it." Anna swept her hand in front of her. Beyond them they could hear the roar of the cars on the motorway. A continuous stream of metallic beetles followed one another over and under, in and out, like a computer game. Little mounds of earth and rubbish, pathetic little corners of newly-planted trees.

They seemed the only living creatures in the landscape.

"This was all ploughed fields, once," Anna sighed.

"And roads," added Martin. "They were always being made, and changed, as the traffic got heavier. Horses, carts and coaches. Dozens of them thundering down those narrow lanes. I bet the locals didn't like them, either. All that straightening and widening of roads, enclosing estates. Do you know I find more bits and pieces to do with horses than anything else. Even coins, and I've got a penny from just after the Norman Conquest."

She eyed him with a new respect. She'd never thought of all those horses.

Anna remembered something.

"Have you been working down by the stream, Martin? A pony's been injured. Caught his fetlock on a piece of metal . . ."

He was genuinely concerned. "I think I know where you mean. No, I haven't been there. Honest. Anyway I wouldn't leave metal lying about. No point. We take it away with us. Otherwise some other person might spend time looking.

"Besides . . . if your Miss B's declared war on us, we'll ask next time. Even if it is a right of way."

"I have to go. I'm late as it is."

"Just a sec. I wanted to ask you. Is this yours?"

The big black key to the tack box lay flat on his hand.

"I didn't pinch it, if that's what you're thinking. You must have dropped it out in the field. It's far too clean to be 'buried treasure'. But it's really old, you know. A hundred and fifty years at least."

Anna thought of the tack box, how secure it was. How solid.

"Made to last." Like friendship perhaps . . . she reached for it.

"See you," she said carelessly.

★ ★ ★

illustration by Claire Colvin

MIDNIGHT STALLION

By Patricia Leitch

I searched for a sign that I would find my way into the world of horses and escape from our bleak life on the farm. When the black stallion arrived I found the sign had always been here...

I used to cut out photographs of Thoroughbred horses, pin them up on my bedroom walls and dream that they were mine; that they grazed in my paddocks and stood in my stables waiting to be saddled, bridled and ridden out over the stretches of sand that lay below our farm.

Sand that reached as far as the eye could see. Sand that was almost white, glistening with a pearl sheen under the moon as the tide drew back – a dancing floor for the white mares of Poseidon.

The mares with manes of foam, who came thundering in night after night as I lay curled in my bed listening to them; white sea-green mares who left no footprints behind them.

I used to search for their hoofprints. Finding them would have been the magical sign I was always seeking. A sign to tell me that I, Kate Flann, was different; that I would not grow up to become a shop assistant or a typist or, worst of all, be trapped in the drudgery of the farm like my mother. Our farm, with its wind-flattened crops, scrawny cattle, decaying walls and leaking roof, was a prison.

I searched for a sign that somehow I would find my way into the world of horses. I would work in racing stables with those high, proud horses.

The speed of them, the blaze of them would be mine. But in our harsh, dead farm I only knew their paper ghosts and no matter how hard I searched I found no magic hoofprints.

The only hoofprints on the sands were those of Peggotty, the farm pony. She was as sour and crabby as the mist that rolled in from the sea, filling our lives with its damp breath.

During the winter my father sat by the kitchen fire, in the summer by the farm door, his bony, lantern-jawed face empty, his flat blue eyes staring inward. Bird-boned as myself, he stretched out his sparrow legs, pulled his cap down over his eyes with delicate, conscious hands and ignored my mother's nagging.

I hardly knew my silent father. He sat drinking black tea, smoking his pipe, crouched over some unspeakable secret from his past, while my mother cleaned and washed, fed beasts and hens and, almost as soon as I had pinned them up, pulled down my paper horses and burnt them.

She would have no such nonsense in her house. Gambling and racing were the devil's playthings. But my favourite horses were hidden from her passionate destruction, only the sea mists knew their rafter security.

Before Tim, my elder brother, abandoned us forever he came into the stable where I was brushing caked mud off Peggotty and told me he was going to sea. I wasn't to tell our parents until he'd gone. He was broad-shouldered and tall like my mother, not a flicker of anything like my father and myself.

A mote-dense beam of sunlight streamed through the broken stable window blotting him out. My eyes were filled with tears at the cruelty of his courage in leaving the farm; his unlikely kindness in telling me he was going. I could hardly see him. I asked my question into a dazzle of light that divided us.

"What did he do?" I asked, feeling the ground tremble, the stable walls collapse about me for I had put into words the question that could not be asked; that must never be mentioned between any of us.

"The old man?" Tim said, as if I could possibly have meant anyone else. His voice was suddenly polite, false, and I was terrified that he wasn't going to tell me.

"What did he do?" I demanded. "Before he came to the farm and married Mam?" The farm had belonged to my mother. Its barren acres, perched on the edge of nowhere, only to be reached by miles of rutted track, had been handed down through four generations of her family.

"It was the horses," said my brother.

"Horses? What was he doing with horses?" I asked, not lifting my eyes.

"Did you not know?" he said knowing that I didn't. "It's the jockey he was before the trouble."

I had not known. Had not known that my father had ridden the bright, blood horses of my dreams.

"Trouble?"

"He was done for doping them. Him and the trainer."

"Prison?"

"He got off. But it finished him. He didn't ride again."

"Was he telling you himself?"

"He was not. It was a bit in an old paper that told me. Guilty it said he was, had it not been for the grand friends that bought him out of it."

Tim had been away for almost a year, when I saw the horsebox coming along the farm track. It was a spring evening with air so sweet that even Peggotty had the breath of it and was allowing herself to be cantered in circles jagged as a rocking horse, but without her usual bouts of bucking and swallow-swooping shies against her ribs.

In the distance of the hilly track the horsebox rose and fell as it came towards the farm. It was a ramshackle thing with wooden sides held together by a cross hatching of planks. Peggotty flung up her head and sent her raucous mare's bray blurting up the cliffside.

From the box came an imperious, dominant answer; a sound I had never heard before.

I took Peggotty's bridle off and then crept slowly round the corner of the hay shed where I could watch the yard without being seen.

Two men were speaking to my father. One was short and stout with a whisky-bloomed face. The other was lean, ginger sharp and although the clothes he wore were faded and folded about his long bones you could see at once there was quality in them.

"It would be for the one night only," said the little, beacon man. "We'll be back for him tomorrow and not a soul the wiser. And for yourself..."

From his pocket he brought out a thick wad of money.

"I will not," said my father. "With the entire police force of Ireland on your trail for all I know."

"Not a one has a breath of us. We have him clean away and not a soul to know that it was himself winning today and not the old crock they thought was running."

"I will not," said my father again and I thought he would turn and leave them.

"It's the short memory you have, Pat Flann," said the tall man.

My mother came to the farm door, stood with her arms folded over her coarse apron. She stood staring at the three men then, without a word, turned and went back inside, slamming the door shut behind herself. From inside the box came the trample of hooves, the high, nickering whinny and then a full-flung explosion of hind feet against the tawdry wood.

"But there's some have not forgotten the money they lost," said the tall, fox-featured man casually. "Some who would still be interested to know where they could find you. And some who could tell them."

They turned and walked away from me so that I couldn't hear what they were saying, but from their backs it looked to me as if the tiny figure of my father stood between two jailers, a prisoner in his own yard. I heard the short man laugh and although my father pushed the wad of notes away I knew from the way the tall man laid his hand on my father's shoulder that he had agreed to do what they wanted.

They backed the box into the dark cell that had once been the bull pen, so I could only hear their captive come crashing down the lowered ramp and the men's voices swearing.

When the men had driven away my father slid the bolt home, padlocked it securely and slipped the key into the breast pocket of his waistcoat.

I went to my room early that night leaving my father crouched over the fire, staring into the flames while my mother sat silently opposite.

I took down my box of paper horses from its rafter hiding place and sitting on my bed I turned over the photographs one by one. I drank them in, lost in their beauty while from the yard below there was the music of trampling hooves, the high, sweet calling. Calling me to come and ride.

It was the early morning before my father's snoring settled into a regular pattern and I knew it was as safe as it would ever be.

I lifted the latch on my bedroom door, and stood barefoot on the landing, my shoes in my hand. My silent feet tested each step of the stairs before I settled my feather weight into the wood.

I crossed the kitchen. Fear of waking my father tightened at my heart as my fingers felt into the egg cup that sat on the left hand corner of the dresser. The padlock key swam into my hand, twin to the one that my father had slipped into his pocket.

A full moon raced motionless through wind-blown clouds as I sat on the back doorstep tying on my shoes. I crossed the yard and took Peggotty's bridle from where I had left it and went slowly, slowly, on to the bull pen where I stood in front of the padlocked doors, the key in my hand.

It was not fear that held me back as I stood on the brink of my miracle. It was a kind of wonder. Not wonder at what was about to happen but wonder that I should ever have been so stupid as to think it might not happen.

I turned the key in the padlock, slid back the bolt and went in, the door closing behind me. The black stallion stood in the far corner, his body lost in darkness. His head, turned towards me, was caught in a net of moonlight that fell through the grill set high in the stone wall, revealing a white blaze, dark ears sharp above a wisped forelock, glistening, moon-mirroring eyes, nostrils trembling with challenge and fine, sensitive lips. As he moved towards me I held out my hand, hardly breathing.

He circled me, neck stretched, silken tail switching about his muscled quarters and over his steel-boned hocks. He aimed one snaking, reaching kick then relaxed. I laid my hand on his neck and it was hard as living rock. I reached to his crested mane and stroked the bulging mass of his shoulder and the plateau of his back. All the time I was talking to him – whispering, words almost without meaning. Only the sound of my voice told him that he came from my dreams.

I took down the rope halter, hooked by the manger – Peggotty's bridle was a useless frivolity. He lowered his head and I slipped it over his ears, secured the rope round his muzzle and, holding him by its length, we went out into the yard and down the track to the beach.

He flaunted at my side, every step he took was tight sprung with energy. Yet he did not trot but kept to his spring-hooved, flirting walk. The track opened to the sea, to a line of breakers far out over moon-blanched sands. For a split second he stood poised, perfectly still, the sea wind bannering back mane and tail, sleeking the moon-shadowed contours of his face. In that second I sprang to his shoulder, and clutching mane and rope I was astride him when he launched into freedom

He reared, landed, flung his hooves in crazed piaffes and caprioles. He advanced to the sea mares, flirting in their wind-blown shadows, blowing into their arching manes. Then the flat, reaching sands took the wildness of his eyes. A limitless racecourse where he could race against only himself and the wind stallions.

I felt his whole being tighten as he drew back the bow of his speed. I knotted rope and silken strands of mane even tighter into my grip. He sprang forward, leaping over space as if the empty night air built barricades before him, then he stretched out, neck low, legs like pistons, his face drawn to the magnetic, invisible rim where sand and sky met.

He showed no sign that he was aware of me as I crouched over his withers like a ghost. It was all a daze of glory, a bursting torrent of unleashed power. Silvered sea and sand skidded past my eyes. I rode free from the bonds of place or time, as I raced against the glimmering moon track that spread its glinting phosphorescent dance over the sea's surface.

A gull flew up out of the darkness and the horse swung round on his hocks and plunged back the way we had come. In that moment all Peggotty's sins were forgiven. It was only due to her twisted, unbroken resistance to all my attempts to school her that I was still astride the horse as he galloped back over his own moon-filled prints.

I was now aware of the world of my father's fury if he found out what I had done. If I had fallen and let the horse gallop loose, what would have happened then? I had to get him back to the farm before anyone found out.

I tried to sit up, to tug at the halter rope, to impose ludicrous control over his speed but he galloped on as if I had never moved. Would I race backwards and forwards over the same stretch of sand until my father discovered us? Again I yanked at the rope, pulling furiously with all my strength but the horse only shook his head, throwing me down onto his neck as he thundered on.

We had almost reached the track to the farm when Peggotty's neighing bray shattered the night silence. The stallion stopped dead, chucking me to the ground. I ran at his side as he trotted up the track towards the sound.

In the yard he stopped and stared about him. His head held high, his white blaze like an uplifted lamp, he screamed into the night. Pathetically I tugged at the halted rope trying to turn him towards the bull pen but he paid as little attention to me as he had when I was on his back.

From the shadows of an outhouse a figure moved towards us. Without a word my father took the halter rope from me and in the instant the horse changed from the mythical, winged horse of my dream to an animal subject to man. He reared against my father's control and fought as he was led back to the prison of the bull pen; but he was an animal and went where he was taken.

My father worked about him, neat and sure in his movements – drying the sweated coat, cleaning legs and hooves, wiping the brilliant face. He spoke to the horse, not to me as I stood silently watching.

When the horse was groomed and pulling at hay he stood back, and I knew that in seconds the heavy doors of the bull pen would be closed and I would never see the horse again. In that moment my mind filled with madness. I would phone the police and tell them that I knew where the horse was; or I would hide in the horsebox, go with the horse to make sure that no harm came to him.

The horse turned his head, looked full at me and in that moment I knew that there was nothing I could ever do for him. In his being he was not only free from his fate at the hands of the men who had brought him here; he was free also from my romantic obsession.

My father shut the doors, bolted and padlocked them. He walked behind me to the farm. At the farm door he paused.

"Be staying in your room," he said, "until the horse is away."

I nodded, opening the door, turning away from him so that he wouldn't see the tears trailing my cheeks.

I was at the foot of the stairs when I heard him catch his breath.

"When the time comes," he said, breaking the silence that had lain between us all my life, "if you still have the notion on you, I'll have a word with a trainer I know. He runs a good straight place and for old time's sake he'll take you on."

By the time I had taken in the meaning of his words, spun round to question him, he was into the kitchen brewing tea for himself, his back set against me.

At odd, sea-strolling moments I still look for the prints of the sea mares but they don't matter now. It didn't really matter when my mother sniffed out my cut-outs hidden in the rafters and threw them on the fire. For I, Kate Flann, have a father who will speak to a trainer for me.

My sign had been with me all the time.

illustration by Steve Humfress

IF WISHES WERE HORSES

By Linda Rostron

When Jenny started to work at Greenacres Stud she soon managed to gain the trust of the horses in her care. But she discovered it wasn't quite so easy to win over Gary, one of the stud assistants...

The sun beat down on Jenny's barely covered shoulders as she studied the notice in the saddler's window:

Full-time help required at Green Acres Stud Farm. Experience with handling horses and basic horse care essential, but further training will be given.

At the bottom of the neatly typewritten notice applicants were asked to contact Sue Johnson at the farm.

Jenny pushed her wavy brown hair away from her hot forehead and continued on her way along the main street.

Jostling with the frantic Friday shoppers, she continued to ponder the advertisement. At sixteen she had experience working at the local riding school and helping with friends' horses, although she had never been in a position to own one. The more she thought about the advert, the more feasible the idea became. Green Acres was within easy cycling distance and summer provided the ideal opportunity to add to her experience of horses.

Deep in thought, she nearly missed her main reason for being in town; the Job Centre. Manoeuvring her way past a harassed mother trying to control her fractious children, the slim girl pushed open the heavy door. The door hinges badly needed oiling and Jenny flushed with embarrassment as the squeaking door temporarily attracted everyone's attention.

Feeling consipicuous, she made her way to the nearest notice board, dotted with a few job adverts, and carefully read through all the possibilities. She took details of one or two without much enthusiasm and was glad to get out in the open again. Sighing and looking at her watch she set off for home.

Jenny was scarcely throught the front door before she was given an ecstatic welcome by Tansy, a three-year-old Labrador. Quivering with excitement, Tansy refused to let the tired girl pass until she had acknowledged her presence.

"Is that you, Jennifer?" Mrs Nichols called from the living room.

"Yes Mum," Jenny replied as she petted Tansy and went into the room.

"Did you have any luck today, dear?" her mother asked.

Nodding, Jenny replied, "I've got a few details for jobs but nothing wonderful."

"At least it's something," Mrs Nichols said optimistically. "You can write some letters after tea."

Frowning with frustration, Jenny put down her pen and went to make some coffee. She found application letters difficult at the best of times, but at the moment she had other things on her mind. The more she thought about the advert in the saddlery, the more appealing it became.

Having carried through two cups of coffee for her mother and herself, Jenny sat down, deep in thought, in front of the television.

"How are you getting on?" Mrs Nichols asked, interrupting Jenny's thoughts. "You've been at those application letters a long time."

"I'm getting through them, slowly, but none of them inspire me with enthusiasm," Jenny replied, absent-mindedly watching the television.

"You have to take what you can get at the moment," her Mum said sadly. "Maybe you'll find something interesting soon".

"I already have," said Jenny, giving her Mum her full attention for the first time and causing her to look more hopeful. Continuing quickly, Jenny said, "There was an advert in the saddlery window. Green Acres wants someone to help." She knew even before she had finished that her Mum was not keen and the silence that followed confirmed it.

Eventually Mrs Nichols said quietly, "Jennifer, you know I want you to get a proper job with a future. I've always tried to make you see that horses can only be a hobby once you have a well-paid job. They're not a job you can rely on".

Jenny knew that what her mother said was true; they needed a reliable income. Her Dad had died in a car crash when she was four so she couldn't really remember him. What she did know, however, was the fact that all their life they had faced an uphill struggle trying to make ends meet.

Jenny's lifelong love of horses meant that she was willing to work for less than she could otherwise earn, but would her mother agree?

"The advert didn't say how much they pay, but the job does have prospects as I would get training," Jenny pleaded.

Again there was a long silence until Mrs Nichols finally conceded.

"It's not the kind of secure future I had hoped you'd have, but as long as you continue with other applications, you can give the stud a try, if they will have you."

Some two weeks later Jenny, feeling rather dispirited, was writing letters and filling in application forms, when a reply arrived from the Green Acres Stud. With great anxiety and trepidation, she opened the letter and read the contents.

She had to read it several times before it finally registered. She was being offered a two-month introductory course and if she proved capable she would be given further training, a pay increase and more permanent position. If convenient she could start the following Monday.

Jenny hurried to show the letter to her mother. Despite the low salary, Mrs Nichols was pleased to see Jenny had recaptured some of her bubbly enthusiasm; the weeks of fruitless job searching had seen a marked change in her. The job would be very welcome, even if only temporarily.

Securing her bike to the white-washed fence, Jenny took a deep breath and opened the gate. A row of looseboxes faced her as she entered the immaculate yard. Shutting the gate carefully, she made her way across the yard. There wasn't a soul to be seen; only the sound of restless horses broke the silence of the morning.

Passing the end stable, Jenny stopped to stroke Midnight Moonshine who was leaning out to see who was about. A lad came round the corner unexpectedly and nearly collided with the unsuspecting girl. Midnight flung up her head in shock as Jenny moved quickly to avoid him. Recovering her balance, she smiled at the brown-haired boy, half-expecting an apology.

Instead, narrowing his eyes and scowling he said, "Who are you? What are you doing here?"

Rather taken aback, Jenny replied politely, "I've come to see Sue Johnson. I'm . . ."

But before she could finished he interruped. "Oh, you must be the *new* girl," putting Jenny in her place before she'd been there five minutes.

"You'll find Sue in the office round the side."

With that he brushed past Jenny and continued on his way, obviously annoyed at having been stopped.

Jenny followed the vague directions, found the office and went in. It was a complete contrast to the tidy stable yard. Papers were strewn untidily over the desk, books on all aspects of horsecare had fallen over each other in the bookcase, cups lay about unwashed and the wall was decorated with numerous photographs of horses.

Two cats purred contentedly on the chair behind the desk and an elderly Alsatian dog padded over to greet her. On hearing the door, a young woman came into the office from the back. With a welcoming smile she said, "You must be Jennifer Nichols? Please sit down." Pushing the cats gently from her chair, she sat down too.

In a friendly manner, Sue introduced the farm and herself. "As you can see, this is only a very small stud, but it has an excellent reputation," she said, pointing towards the photographs lining the wall. She described the routine and how Jenny would fit in. There were only two other permanent staff, Louise and Gary.

When Jenny remarked that she'd already met Gary, Sue commented, "You may find him a bit sharp but he's very good with the horses."

Sue then showed Jenny round. Behind the stables stretched green fields in which foals ran together full of the joys of life or bullied their mothers to play. The horses she was to help look after included Midnight, who was due to foal in a month's time.

The first two weeks passed quickly. The work was hard but she thoroughly enjoyed it and became firm friends with Louise, a quiet, friendly girl. So far Jenny had seen little of Gary...

Jenny waited as Louise opened the stable door and led the brood mare in. The two-week-old foal shoved against its mother's flanks, determined not to be left even a few millimetres behind. Watching the mare nudge her son in assurance, Jenny left the stable and Louise bolted the door behind her. After making sure the pair had settled, the two girls set about their daily tasks.

A little later, Jenny jumped as Gary bellowed across the yard for

Louise. Thinking something dreadful must have happened, she dropped what she was doing and hurried to help. What she saw was Gary, holding the mare by the headcollar with the foal attempting to merge into her side, and a very upset Louise.

Gary was shouting. "I thought I could trust you and that girl to bring Minty in. Obviously I can't," he raged. "I don't expect to come into the yard and find valuable animals running loose. I didn't think you were too incompetent to bolt the stable door!".

Seeing that Louise was very near to tears and that she couldn't even get a word in edgeways to defend herself, Jenny stepped forward to speak up for her.

"Louise did bolt the door. I was there," she said.

Noticing Jenny for the first time, Gary's eyes narrowed in annoyance at this contradiction. His fingers clenched and his knuckles turned white. Minty shifted uneasily, sensing his anger and not knowing whether or not it was directed at her.

"Then," he demanded, barely controlling his patience, "how did Minty get out? You girls would stick together." Before either could reply, Gary returned mother and son to the stable. With exaggerated carefulness he shot the bolt shut as if to show how it should be done.

Before he had gone far, there was a rattle of the bolt and all eyes turned to see Minty working it open with her teeth. Colour rising to his cheeks, Gary turned to see Jenny's knowing smile and looking her straight in the eye he said, "You think you know everything now you've been here for three weeks, but I assure you, you'll soon find you don't!"

A few days later Jenny met Gary as she was leading the Arab stallion out to the paddocks.

"Where are you taking Sultan?" he asked.

"I'm turning him out in the second field," Jenny replied, trying to be pleasant.

Gary paused for a minute and then, without explanation, ordered, "Put him in the fourth field instead."

When Jenny went to bring in Sultan several hours later, she thought that the flies were bothering him. He was standing in the middle of the field, glancing uncomfortably at his stomach. Then suddenly he threw himself on the ground and rolled.

Jenny's heart started to thump. It looked like colic. Shouting for someone to get the vet, she hurried over to the stallion and clipped the leading rein onto his headcollar just as the sweating animal got to his feet. Trying desperately to stop him rolling again, Jenny headed towards the gate. Three concerned faces met them as they entered the yard. "The vet is on his way," said Sue. "Keep him moving but don't tire him out."

It seemed an eternity before he arrived and Sultan was taken into a loosebox for examination. Sue went with the vet while everyone else waited anxiously outside. Jenny wondered why Gary looked so white and seemed to avoiding catching her eye, but she had more important matters on her mind.

Sue eventually came out of the loosebox. "Sultan should be OK now. Louise, could you make sure he doesn't catch a chill as he cools down?" she said and, turning back to her office added, "Jenny, I'd like a word, please".

As soon as she entered the office, the worried girl could tell that Sue was angry.

"You were in charge of Sultan, so why on earth did you turn him out into that field?" Before Jenny could explain, she continued, "Your stupidity nearly lost us a very valuable animal. That field has not been grazed yet and the grass is exceptionally lush. Horses should only be turned out there for very short periods, not all afternoon. By rights you deserve the sack but I know how hard you have worked here. Although I can't forget this, I'm willing to give you a second chance."

Seizing the opportunity, Jenny said, "But it was Gary who told me to put him in that field"

"Gary has been here much longer than you and would not have done such a stupid thing. You must have misheard him," replied Sue. Before Jenny could protest further she added, "Now I think you'd better get on with your work before I change my mind."

Seeing that it was pointless to say anything more, Jenny left the office, realising now why Gary wouldn't meet her eyes. She couldn't believe that he would have risked the life of an animal, deliberately, to get his own back on her.

Very early one morning the telephone rang insistently in the Nichols' home. A sleepy Jenny answered it but she was soon jolted wide awake. It was Gary. When she heard what he had to say she threw on some clothes, grabbled her bike and pedalled furiously to the stud.

Sue had been called away suddenly and left Gary in charge. He met her at the gate. Without a word he headed towards Midnight's stable.

Through the dim light, they could tell that Midnight was beginning to get distressed. Something was wrong. The mare grunted frequently and her swelling sides heaved but there was no sign of the foal. Panic rose within Jenny but she forced it down again as she knew the mare would sense it and panic herself.

Praying that the vet would arrive soon, she put her faith in Gary, who had seen many mares foal. Gary, by now, was in the stable. Kneeling down next to the mare, he soothed her. He then moved to help with the foal. For the first time Jenny realised why he was so valued at the stud and why Sue had said 'he's good with the horses'.

Motioning Jenny to the mare's head to encourage her, Gary altered the foal's position, quickly and gently, whilst speaking reassuringly to the mare.

Jenny was surprised by his confidence and expertise. Once the foal was in the correct position it only needed a few more heaves from Midnight and it was born. Speaking a few words of praise to the mare, Jenny fetched a bucket of warm water and cleared the nose and mouth of the tiny foal.

As the filly attempted to stand on its long, weak legs, the mare began to clean her, sending her sprawling once again in a heap on the thickly padded floor. Both Gary and Jenny laughed and for the first time since Jenny started at the stud, a look of friendship passed between them.

The vet arrived soon after and was pleased to find things had gone well. Within a couple of hours the foal was standing and feeding, its small, spiky mane beginning to show. Casting a last glance at the pair, Jenny collected her bike and headed home for a few hours' sleep.

Spirit of Dawn, as the foal was aptly named, proved to be a boisterous little filly full of fun and courage.

While she was cleaning the mare and foal's stable, Jenny began to wonder what would happen when her trial period was up. Would it be back to applying for more conventional jobs? The possibility of working in a stuffy office now seemed even more unbearable.

Interrupting these thoughts, Louise told Jenny that Sue wanted to see her in her office. When she got there Gary was also present.

"We have been discussing your future," Sue said and Jenny's heart sank as she realised that Gary would take this opportunity to get rid of her. "We have both been impressed by your work with the horses and the way you coped with Midnight. Although you have made mistakes we have decided to offer you a permanent position at Green Acres".

Jenny was speechless. That was the last thing she had expected. Barely able to control her mounting excitement, she accepted eagerly the offer. She was on the point of leaving the room when Gary, much to her surprise, said, "I think I owe you an apology, Jenny. I shouldn't have told you to put Sultan in that field. I didn't think the grass was so lush and didn't expect Sultan to be so affected. I'm sorry."

When Sue recovered from the shock of this admission, she said, "Could you get on with what you were doing, please, Jenny? I would like to speak to Gary alone".

When Gary came out of the office he smiled sheepishly at Jenny and said, "That was the first time she's really told me off since I started and I hope it's the last!"

Cycling home, Jenny smiled to herself with pleasure. She was finally doing something she had longed to do all her life – work with horses. Sue had decided to keep Spirit and Jenny was to help bring her on. When she was seventeen, Jenny hoped to take the Stud Assistants' Exam and head for the Diploma. Things were definitely going her way...

★ ★ ★

illustration by Claire Colvin

JOKER'S PROMISE

By Fliss Gillott

Lucy fell in love with Joker the minute she set eyes on him. She promised Jack, his owner, she would be back next summer to see the cheeky foal and his mother, Rosie, again. But before she could return Joker's secure world was shattered...

Every day, Jack would walk the two miles from his home to see his mare and foal. He wished he could own a house with a paddock so they could be with him all the time. It worried him that, but for the hour he spent leaning over the field gate, they were left unattended.

He was an old man but he counted himself lucky. He had his own little house which wasn't too far from this well-sheltered field in a quiet lane. This way he could keep his old mare in her retirement with what would be her last foal.

As he stood and watched one day, Rosie wandered over and lifted her head to nuzzle his face. Jack delved into the pocket of his jacket and produced a couple of ripe apples.

"Here you are, old girl, eat up! You deserve a little treat. You've got us a fine colt this year. He's going to be a real champion, that one!"

Jack and Rosie had been together for almost all of her twenty years, since he bought her for fifteen pounds in Cambridge market. Then she was a scrawny, louse-ridden reject, all hair and wild eyes. But even then, there was something about the way she moved that caught his eye. He had a liking for coloured horses, skewbald or piebald, it didn't really matter.

The spring in her step made her look all legs and in spite of her appearance she had a proud and defiant bearing. He had no trouble buying her; nobody else was interested.

It took nearly a year to bring out her trust in him. She grew a little but made only just under fifteen hands. Jack broke her to saddle and later to harness so she could pull a little flat cart for him. With this, Jack and Rosie went round the local farms and houses collecting junk.

Twice before, when Jack had had a bit of luck picking up a few good bargains, Rosie was given a year off work to have a foal. This colt was her third and Jack knew he was the best. The colt, like Rosie, had a defiant look in his eye and a spring in his step. He was by far her biggest foal and certainly the fastest. She was very proud of this son.

"Are they your horses?"

Jack turned to see a mousey-haired girl had joined him at the gate.

"Yep."

"What's their names?"

"Rosie and – dunno, haven't thought yet."

"Can I give him a name then?"

"Well, yes I s'pose you can. How old are you?"

"Ten and a half."

"What are you doing out on your own at your age?"

"I'm staying with my aunt. She doesn't mind. She lets me come and see the horses. I love horses. I wish I had my own. Can I call him Joker? He's really funny!"

The colt by this time was galloping flat out, round and round the field, like a huge puppy. Every now and again he would give a little buck and then spin effortlessly round to gallop the other way. In spite of his long legs, he was beautifully balanced and could stop in a moment as though he had never moved at all. As the little girl spoke he arrived at his mother's side with a babyish snort. He stood motionless and looked straight at her, his ears pricked forward.

Jack laughed. "He likes the name I reckon! Not the first to be called Joker but – yeah, okay. Joker he is. What's your name then?"

"Lucy."

"Lucy and Joker. You make a good pair!"

"I've got to go now. Can I come again? Can I come tomorrow? Can I bring Joker some sugar?"

"You're a proper chatterbox for a littl'un, you are. Yeah, come tomorrow, same time but no sugar."

"Ooh, thank you," she gasped and ran off.

"Funny kid," thought Jack, "but she seems nice enough. Be good to have someone to chat to."

The next day and the days after that Lucy was always there when Jack arrived. He showed her how to stroke Joker's nose without frightening him or upsetting Rosie. The four soon became firm friends. Lucy learnt to respect Joker when he was playing. Sometimes he would kick out at her as though playing with another foal and it was only Jack's sharp reactions that kept the child out of trouble.

Soon she was able to scratch the side of his neck and watch his little whiskery top lip curl up with sheer pleasure at her touch. Every day he was growing bigger and looking more like a horse than the gangly foal he had first been.

Lucy was hopelessly in love with him.

It was a warm Sunday morning when Jack found her crying into a grubby pink tissue outside the field.

"Hey, Titch, what's up?"

"I've got to go home tonight. Back to London. I'll never see Joker again! He'll forget me and I love him! He's the best foal in the world! What can I do? I think I'll run away! Oh, Jack, what can I do?"

"Stop all that at once!" said Jack sternly. "He'll be here next year. I'm not selling 'im. He won't forget. You're special to Joker. Horses remember their friends. And if you think he's the best in the world, then learn to ride and come back and prove it."

"Okay Jack, I'll be back next June, after school. You wait and see! I won't let you and Rosie and Joker down. You'll see."

With that, she was gone. Jack missed her company. Rosie was content enough. She had Jack and the colt, plenty to eat and room to move, fresh air and the sun on her back. Life was good.

When Lucy returned a year later, they had all gone. No Jack, no Rosie and, worst of all, no Joker.

As the summer of Lucy's visits turned to autumn, Rosie's and Joker's coats started to thicken. Jack had started bringing them hay on his daily visits and Rosie looked forward eagerly to his arrival. One day, he didn't come. She paced up and down by the gate for two hours but as darkness fell she gave up, wandering off to graze once more. Joker didn't mind so much, he could always get a warm, nourishing feed from his mother. The next day, the same thing happened. Jack still didn't appear. Rosie was worried, but could do nothing. The days passed slowly but there was no sign of her friend.

Gradually, the worry and lack of food started to show in Rosie's condition. Everything she was eating was going to Joker. Her udder, even now, was always full. She was losing the round, healthy look along her neck and over her quarters, while her ribs started to push against the skin under her thickening coat. As the tastiest grass was all gone, she started to feed on the coarse grass which grew in odd places and to nibble at the hedge.

Resigned to this new way of life, her only pleasure was in watching Joker cavorting about whenever he felt in the mood. Had she been younger, she might have joined in with his zany games but her joints were beginning to get stiff and painful. Rosie was tired too. Always tired.

"Go on, I dare you to get on!" shouted a strange voice. It was nearly dark. Who was it? Rosie was alarmed. She didn't understand the words, yet something made her feel uneasy.

"No, you catch it first! You said you could ride a horse!"

"Alright, come on then, give us a hand. We'll get it in a corner!" Rosie whipped round. Where was Joker? He whinnied from the other side of the field, sensing something was wrong. Suddenly, Rosie realised she was surrounded by a crowd of strange people. Joker was behind them, rushing back and forth, trying to get to his mother.

Rosie trotted forward a few steps and felt herself grabbed by rough hands, loud voices shouting from all directions. Somebody had got hold of her nose, there were strong fingers pressing into her nostrils. She tried to shake them off, but it was too late. Everything seemed to happen at once, the tight string all round her head, a figure leaping onto her back, heels kicking her sides, voices, shouting. Joker, where was he? In terror, she struck out with her front legs and then kicked out behind her, trying desperately to buck and get away from her captors.

There was a sudden scream of pain.

"Get a stick or something, beat her up! The old cow's kicked me!"

"Yeah, go on, give her a thrashing! If she wants a fight she can have one!"

Rosie's heart was pounding. She could feel nothing but fear, fear for herself and fear for her foal. Her legs were giving way with each step she took, her feet were catching on the ground until eventually she stumbled and fell.

"Come on, let's go. I've had enough of this. This old crate's no fun any more."

"Yeah, come on lads, let's beat it. She don't look too good to me!"

They were alone again. Rosie and Joker. Where was Jack, oh where was he? Rosie's lungs were straining painfully as she gasped for air. All night she had stood where the boys had left her, dripping with sweat and blood from the many small cuts which covered her body. Still her sides heaved with the effort of breathing and still her heart pounded painfully in her chest. Joker bent to push his nose under her for a warm, comforting feed but she didn't move a muscle; she barely noticed.

Joker had met nothing but kindness and love before this fateful night. Now he knew fear and hate. He stayed close to Rosie, sharing the warmth of his body. He was hungry and thirsty but couldn't leave her. As night drew in again, he could bear it no longer, his thirst took him to the water trough on the far side of the field. Having drunk his fill he went back to his mother. This time, she was down, flat on her side, head stretched out on the cool grass.

"Joker," she said, "take care of yourself." Horses may not speak as we do, in words, but their own silent language is just as full of meaning and emotion as ours. Joker understood everything she said to him.

"Mother, why?"

"If only I knew, if only. Remember Jack and Lucy, they are good people. Be on your guard, Joker. Trust your instincts. Don't trust blindly, Joker!"

"Mother, please get up!" Joker pushed Rosie with his nose and pawed the ground. "Please mother, get up!"

Rosie lay still. She never moved again.

Several days passed. Joker was lonely and afraid. Just seven months old, he was far from ready to cope with life without the guidance of an older companion. No horse ever likes to be alone, but for a youngster of Joker's tender years the terrible isolation was almost overpowering.

Sometimes, in the distance he heard hooves clattering along a road or the neighing of an unseen horse. Could he find help on his own? He was getting increasingly hungry too. His body was telling him to go in search of food, yet the presence of his dead mother was holding him like a magnet.

He found himself wandering nearer and nearer to the gate where Jack used to appear with hay and apples or carrots. He didn't expect to see Jack any more but instinct told him this was the direction he had to take. The intruders had left the gate half open. Trembling with fear but desperate for help, Joker stepped cautiously into the road.

Away to the right, he had heard the sounds of the other horses and this was where his faltering steps were leading him. Once he was on strange ground, he broke into a trot, his eyes darting this way and that, sensing unseen danger.

The lane led out onto a main road. Joker was used to the sight and sound of an occasional passing car and they held no fear for him. But he was not prepared for this sudden rush of traffic. With no instincts to guide him he went straight out across the busy road.

All hell seemed to break loose. Horns hooted, engines roared, brakes squealed. Joker was terrified! He took off in a headlong gallop, swerving left and right to find a way out of this mad, deafening uproar until – BANG! Something hit him. He felt himself spin into the air and he landed with a thud on the grass verge.

People came rushing over from all directions but poor Joker hardly noticed. He didn't want to move, he didn't want to try.

"Clear a space please. Move along, come on. The vet's here. Stand back everybody!"

"Let me through, I'm a vet."

"Are you going to shoot him?"

"Not unless I have to. Alright, little horse. Help is here."

The vet's voice was soothing. As he chatted quietly and stroked Joker's neck and shoulders, the colt's mind slowly started to come back into focus. Without warning his legs flailed.

"Whoa, boy, whoa, steady, steady!" The young vet realised his wounded patient had one thing in mind – flight – and he couldn't let him get away. He was badly wounded and he had to be kept away from the traffic.

"Help me keep his head down 'til we can get a headcollar on him! Come on, give me a hand – anybody! Quick, there's one in my car!" Several pairs of hands worked quickly to get the headcollar on Joker, then he was allowed to struggle to his feet.

"Would you believe it! Looks as though nothing's broken!"

"Don't speak too soon. We can't really tell without cleaning him up and examining him thoroughly. I'll need help to get him to the surgery. Who owns him?"

The policeman stepped over. "Can't trace him Mr Wright. I've called the station and they're following it up. Do you want to take him in? With his colouring, he's probably gypsy stock. May not get your bills paid, you know that don't you?"

The vet smiled sadly. "I can't worry about that now. Look at him. He's a mess but he's not finished. No I've got to do what I can. Let's get transport sorted out for him and clear this road. The sooner the better."

Joker's luck had returned; he'd fallen into the hands of a very caring and capable group of people. During that first week, he was tended every night and day.

Joker had never been in a stable before. It looked and smelt strange and did nothing to boost his will to live. It was the kind words and gentle touch which kept him alive. Those were things he had known before.

His injuries weren't as bad as they might have been. He was very badly bruised and had some dreadful wounds but no broken bones. Simon was pleased with the progress he was making.

"He's a fighter, this one, Mary!"

"That's as maybe but he's also very sweet natured. Have you noticed, he hasn't threatened us once and we must have hurt him?"

"You know that mare that was found in the field in Back Lane? I reckon that's where he came from. Whatever happened to her would have scared him half to death. Could be why he was on the run."

"Yes, you could be right," said Mary the nurse thoughtfully, "but somebody at some time must have shown him kindness. Otherwise he would never have trusted us."

"Yes, it's a bit of a mystery. Looks as though I've got myself a permanent resident unless they find out who owned the mare."

"Simon, what about taking him for a walk? It's a week now and he seems strong."

"Okay . . . I'll give you a hand."

Between them Brian and Mary persuaded a very stiff and sore Joker to venture out of his stable. It was a turning point for him. Once he felt his muscles starting to ease, his old spirit began to return. Day by day, he was taken a little further round the yard. It wasn't long before he gave his first playful buck. Mary was delighted! She asked Simon's permission to let him run free. His new field wasn't exactly big, it was more like a grassy yard, but to Joker it was paradise. He was still very lame so after a brief and quite comical skip round, he put his head down to eat and eat and eat.

By spring, Joker had grown into a tall, handsome, healthy yearling. His wounds had healed. He was scarred but sound. Simon was very proud of him.

The police had managed to trace Jack through the owner of the field, so at least Simon knew where he came from. Jack had had a bad stroke which left him almost completely paralysed and unable to speak. He couldn't possibly look after Joker so Simon was allowed to keep the colt as payment for the work he had done.

Lucy, meanwhile, had been busy at home in London. Now that she so badly wanted to learn to ride, she spent most of her time doing odd jobs for neighbours and friends. All this extra pocket money went in a round sweet tin with a slot in the top which she kept under her bed. This was to be her riding money. All she ever talked about now was horses.

She was surprised to find a letter addressed to 'Miss Lucy Archer' in Auntie Vera's handwriting waiting for her one day when she got back from school. She sat down on a stool in the kitchen and tore open the envelope.

"Dear Lucy," she read.

"I have some rather sad news for you. Now don't get too upset, it's not all bad! I'm sorry to say that, although your Joker is perfectly well, Rosie (have I got the name right?) is no longer with us. I seem to remember you said she was very old and from what I hear, she just passed away in her field. If she had to go then that seems the best way, doesn't it?

"In case you're wondering how I know, I'll tell you. You remember Mrs Meakin who runs the Post Office? Your friend Jack also goes in

there, so she knows him too. This is the other bit of bad news. He's not too well as he had a stroke. This means he can't really move one side of his body at the moment and he can't speak properly.

"Anyway. Mrs Meakin told me that a young horse had got out on the main road and caused a fair bit of chaos. It took the police ages to find out where he came from because, of course, Jack couldn't tell anyone that his horses needed looking after. It was the man who owns the field who found the colt's mother and then they all put two and two together. I think he owns a bean canning factory doesn't he? Not that it matters much but one of his workers knows Mrs Meakin you see,that's how I know!

"I expect you're dying to know about your beloved Joker aren't you dear? Well, he's fine. According to Mrs Meakin, he's now living with Mr Wright the vet and doing very nicely. If you like, I'll give him a ring. Maybe he'd let you go and visit when you come here in June.

"Well, there you are! I'm sorry to have to tell you all this bad news. I hope you still want to come and see me in June. It's so nice to have you around. The cats and I are very well, anyway and we miss you! Look after yourself, dear and if you have time, write to me soon.

Lots of love,

Auntie Vera."

By the time she had finished reading, Lucy's cheeks were wet with tears. She read the letter again and again, hardly able to believe that Rosie was gone and Jack was ill. Lucy was no letter writer but on this occasion she was quick to reply. In a rather untidy scrawl she wrote –

"Dear Auntie Vera,

Thank you for finding all this out for me. I want to see Joker and Jack please and I wouldn't not come to stay with you for all the world.

See you on June 25th.

Love,

Lucy"

Together, Lucy and her aunt went to see Joker. Lucy leant on the field gate and called his name. It never crossed her mind that he might have forgotten her. He lifted his head at the sound of her voice, whinnied noisily and cantered towards her. Something about Lucy reminded him of happy, carefree days, security and contentment.

Having seen Joker and spent a happy morning watching him graze and fool around, Lucy found it easier than she thought to visit Jack.

She was able to chat away as she had the previous summer, just as though little had changed. For Jack, the visit was like a tonic. The faint whiff of horses that came into his hospital room from Lucy's clothes, together with her cheerful chatter, brought back happy memories and he rested well that night.

He knew now that it was only a question of time before he could tell her the whole story of how Joker came into being.

"Some day," he thought to himself, "I'm going to make sure that little Lucy makes my colt into the champion he was born to be!". . .

illustration by Steve Humfress

SAVING UP

By Anna Baness

Philippa knew exactly what her dream pony would look like – she was drawing him bit by bit. But then she had to ride Snowstorm in a scavenge hunt and learnt that real life can be just as good as dreams...

Philippa worked quickly and skilfully until the outline of her dream pony lay on the paper in front of her. He was tall with an arched neck and an elegant head. He would have a long, black, flowing mane and tail . . .

Philippa checked herself and put the pencil down resignedly on the table. You could not draw the outline of something that would move like a real pony. No, it would just have to wait until she could do it properly with brushes and paint. When that would be she did not know.

Now came the hard part. She was going to ruin her drawing for the moment by ruling straight lines across it. First, one between each hoof and leg, then one between each leg and the body. Finally even the body and head were divided into neat portions. Philippa stared at her drawing sadly. "I wonder when, if ever, you'll be a whole pony again," she murmered. "If you stay a divided pony it means I won't have saved enough for a real pony."

Two pots of paint, two brushes, a jar of water and a tin lay on the table beside her. Philippa picked up the tin and opened it. Inside were several notes and a layer of silver and copper coins. Slowly and carefully she counted the money, placing it in rows of neat little piles. She sighed when she had finished. It seemed such a pitifully small sum, but maybe it was just enough to allow her to paint in an eye.

She opened the pot of brown paint and dipped the finer of the two brushes into it. Then very carefully she painted in a delicate brown eye. The water in the jam jar went cloudy as she dipped her brush in.

"That's all Philippa," she told herself. "It's all you can allow yourself to do until you have saved up some more money."

She found some drawing pins and pinned up the picture carefully on her cork memo board opposite the bed. The pony was a dim shape on the white paper but the eye watched her. Philippa looked at it.

"I will save," she said, "I'll save and save until I can paint you, your head, your neck, oh all of you and then I'll give you a beautiful black mane and tail."

"Philippa, Philippa," her mother called and she hurried out of her bedroom and down the stairs.

"I'm just going shopping," Mrs Craven said. "Do you want to

come?"

Philippa was silent for a moment. Going shopping meant spending money, the precious money she was saving for a pony. On the other hand . . .

They went out into the street together, Mrs Craven striding along with a large shopping basket in one hand and an elderly black umbrella in the other. She used the umbrella as a hill walker might use a stick, spiking it down onto the pavement at each stride. She never went out without her umbrella because she would not take the slightest risk about the weather.

"Now I'm just going into this store. Was it something in here you wanted?" Mrs Craven asked, stopping to wait for her daughter.

"No," Philippa shook her head as she looked through the large window of the supermarket.

"Well you go off and buy what you want, then meet me here in half an hour," her mother said.

Philippa set off at a purposeful trot towards the ironmongers.

At the back of the shop were towers of buckets, all shapes, sizes and colours. Household buckets, builders' buckets and yes, there they were, the cut-price black buckets like the ones used at the stables. Philippa stared at them happily, imagining the day her dream pony would be reality and she would carry his water to him in one of these.

"Can I help you?" the man asked.

"Yes please, I would like that bucket there," Philippa said, pointing to one a third of the way down the pile.

"Is it for a pony?" he asked.

"Yes." Philippa paused then added, "Well at least it will be when I get him."

She handed over the money, took the change and skipped out of the shop.

Mrs Craven was waiting for her daughter outside the supermarket. She raised her eyebrows as Philippa approached along the pavement, swinging her bucket.

"Marion is coming home this afternoon. She said she'd drive you up to the stables tonight," her mother said.

"Oh lovely," Philippa cried, running along the pavement.

Marion had been adopted by the Cravens five years before Philippa was born. She had left home now and was working as a dressage groom.

That evening Philippa sat beside Marion and listened entranced to her horsy stories as they drove towards the stables.

"I hear you're entering your first competition soon," Marion remarked as they turned into the car park behind the stable yard.

"Oh yes but it's only a scavenge hunt," Philippa paused for a moment. "We're being allotted ponies tonight."

"That'll be exciting."

"Well I'm not sure, you see there's this pony called Snowstorm who twitches and dithers so much you can't even mount sometimes. Emily thinks I'm going to have him."

"Well Emily might be wrong and if she's not you'd probably find this Snowstorm was the best of the lot," Marion said.

"I don't know," Philippa was dubious.

They climbed out of the car and walked through the stable yard to the indoor school. The school ponies were all stabled in a line inside the large building.

"Which is Snowstorm?" Marion asked as they went in through the sliding doors.

"He's down there. I do hope I might win so I can paint the face," Philippa said.

"What face?" Marion was puzzled.

"Oh the face on my drawing," Philippa replied and went on to explain about her savings.

Marion listened thoughtfully as they walked down the line of ponies to see Snowstorm. She remembered all her own plans for saving; the knotted sock that had been supposed to look like a horse's head and the jam jars and tins all labelled with parts of the horse.

"So this is the pony you think will ruin all your hopes," she said, looking at the little grey gelding with a flowing mane and tail.

"Yes."

Marion put out her hand to pat his neck.

"Don't touch his mane, it makes him go all twitchy," Philippa said quickly.

"Does it boy?" Marion said, stroking his nose. "I think you're rather lovely, yes I do."

"You wouldn't if you had to ride him. Oh I do hope . . ."

Philippa broke off and her brow furrowed.

It was not until after the lesson that the instructor told them who they would be riding for the scavenge hunt. Philippa had been riding especially well, hoping she would be given Brandy, an elegant chestnut who was supposed to be very fast.

". . . and Philippa, I think you can have Snowstorm as you are obviously well able to cope with him now . . ." the instructor said.

Of course Philippa smiled, because any pony is better than no pony at all, but underneath she was feeling angry, anxious and disappointed all at once.

"I knew it, oh I knew it," she said, flopping into the passenger seat of Marion's car.

"Come on now, it isn't the end of the world," Marion said cheerfully.

"But I won't even have a chance of winning," Philippa cried.

"I don't know, I rather liked him. I tell you what, would you let me be one of your helpers then we can show the others how wrong they all are about him?" Marion asked.

"Would you, would you really?" Philippa's face was alight with excitement again. "Mother can be the other helper, you're allowed two you see."

"Right, that's settled then."

It was a week until the scavenge hunt. On the Monday Philippa found her best jodhpurs, polished her boots and whip, brushed over the velvet on her hat and ironed a white shirt. Each day she checked that everything was tidy and ready.

On Friday evening Philippa ran all the way home from school. She arrived breathlessly in the kitchen as Marion was putting the kettle on for tea.

"Hello, practising for tomorrow?" she asked, looking amused.

"Practising?" Philippa was puzzled.

"Yes for all the running you'll have to do."

"Will I?"

"You might," Marion said flicking her short, dark hair out of her eyes and smiling.

Marion knew how she felt, remembering the days of preparation for those first shows and events that always seemed to be over all too quickly.

The next morning Philippa was awake very early. Dim light filtered through her curtains and she lay and looked at her drawing on the wall. The eye stared back at her challengingly.

"Perhaps, oh just perhaps, I'll be able to paint your face tonight," Philippa whispered.

It seemed a long, long time until she heard movements in the rest of the house and knew that she could at last get dressed. She jumped out of bed and ran across her room to the neat pile of clothes. She was just pulling on her jodhpurs when she thought about egg stains and reluctantly took them off again.

"Feeling fit?" Marion asked as they sat down to breakfast.

"I hope so. Do you think I stand any chance of winning anything? After all I've never been in a scavenge hunt before," Philippa said.

"Well I haven't seen the opposition but I should think you stand every chance of getting a prize," Marion said cheeringly.

The scene at the riding stables was one of subdued excitement when they arrived. Philippa looked round her happily, then looked across at her mother and smiled.

"Let's go and get Snowstorm ready," Marion said, leading the way towards the indoor school.

All the school ponies were being brushed 'til they shone by their respective riders.

They walked down behind the line of ponies and found Snowstorm.

"Do you think he'll let us groom him or will it make him go all twitchy?" Philippa asked.

"We'll soon see, won't we boy. I'll give you a proper strapping, shall I?" Marion said, patting the little grey pony and beginning to brush his shoulder.

Philippa took a body brush and began on his mane and tail. They worked together until his coat was gleaming and his mane and tail hung like spun silver.

"There, you can put the hoof oil on," Marion said, standing up straight again and cleaning the brushes.

Ten minutes later they were waiting with all the other competitors in the stable yard while the list of articles to be found was handed to each rider sealed in an envelope. The ponies were already restless, jostling and pawing the ground.

"Alright you may start now," their instructor shouted.

Marion watched Philippa tear open the envelope with eager fingers. She could see the excitement in her face. Snowstorm was restless and suddenly he shied sideways, pulling against Marion.

"Whoa boy, easy," she said, patting his neck and feeling the quiver of excitement run through him.

Other ponies were already leaving the yard and Marion turned Snowstorm to follow them.

"Come on, read as you go along and shout when you want me to stop," she said, beginning to run.

It was difficult to read when the paper moved up and down, Marion knew from experience. But that was all part of a scavenge hunt.

Hooves clattered up the lane behind them and suddenly they were part of a mass of eager ponies all racing to find the things first.

A holly leaf ... there were five ponies by the tree, a twig in someone's eye, a yelp of pain then Philippa's triumphant voice urging Snowstorm on again.

Marion was breathless from the hill but she kept running already, as determined as Philippa not to let the bay pony behind them come past.

A pebble, an old bottle and still the bay was just behind.

"Oh it's Amy," Philippa cried suddenly. "Run Marion."

"I am running, what's next?"

"A conker."

They all knew where the horse chestnut tree was and Marion

heard the clatter of many hooves behind them. Down the lane again, across the car park and there it was.

"Oh that's mean," Philippa cried when she found she could not reach even the lowest conkers.

The lower branches of the tree had been cut off and now the leaves rustled tantalisingly just out of reach.

Mrs Craven looked up from a fruitless search on the ground and suddenly they were surrounded by other ponies.

"How are we going to get one?" Philippa cried, looking round for inspiration.

Suddenly her eye fell on her mother's umbrella.

"Quick Mum, your umbrella!"

Mrs Craven handed it to her and Philippa triumphantly hooked down a branch and picked one fat, green chestnut.

Snowstorm swung round, eager to go again, and Marion ran beside him. But other ponies were also leaving the tree. Suddenly the bay shot past them.

"Amy's overtaken us," Philippa cried, urging Snowstorm on with her heels.

Down the lane to find some sheep's wool and suddenly they were on their own. No hooves thundered behind them and the shouts of excitement died away.

"They can't all have finished, can they?" Philippa asked nervously.

"No of course not," but even Marion was not sure; where was everyone else?

While Philippa dismounted and mounted again Snowstorm stood like a rock – a thing unheard of before.

"I told you he was a good pony really," Marion said as they clattered back up the lane.

Philippa was not listening; she was looking round for the other competitors. Suddenly she saw them strung out across a field searching for things in the grass.

"There they are," she cried in relief.

Mrs Craven found the last few things in the hedge and suddenly they were heading for the door of the indoor school. They were nearly there when the little bay appeared from the other direction at a canter. Snowstorm bit the offending pony's tail as he shot through the door just ahead of them.

Marion steadied the excited pony and grinned.

"Well done, you're second!" called their instructor.

That evening Philippa took down her drawing and found paint and brushes. She opened the pot of brown paint and stared at it, she picked up the brush and put it down again. Suddenly even the picture seemed wrong.

"He's not like that," she muttered to herself. "My dream pony is a grey now, a grey like . . . like Snowstorm."

She found another piece of paper, a black piece, and re-drew the outline of a pony. Then, picking up her brush, she dipped it into the white paint and began to paint his beautiful, kind face, smiling as she worked.

illustration by Claire Colvin

THE RUNAWAY

By Carol Vaughan

When Valerie's world came crashing down the ponies at Unicorn Stables were her one consolation. But Valerie's nerve for riding had deserted her, until one day a top-class showjumper helped to bring it back...

Valerie Jones had just finished sweeping the yard when the last Saturday afternoon class returned. The ponies were snatching at their bits and shoving, eager for their feeds and to be rid of riders and tack. Leaning her broom against the wall, Valerie walked over to help some of the younger riders; at fifteen she was more than a match for impatient ponies.

"It was super," said one small rider. "You should have come too, Val. Why don't you ever ride with us?"

Valerie turned away without answering. She had asked herself the same question too many times. Marina Barker, the red-headed know-it-all, dismounting from her own pony, Gallant, kept at livery at the stables, answered for her.

"Val doesn't ride with the likes of us," she said sarcastically. "Once she was good, then she lost her nerve, so now she doesn't ride at all. Even the quietest pony gives her the shakes. *I* always thought you had to remount straight away, after a bad fall."

"You look after Gallant," said Miss Denison, the owner of the Unicorn Stables, curtly. "When you are perfect, you can start minding other people's business; right now, you'd be well advised to mind your own. You've galloped Gallant into a lather again." Sulkily, Marina dragged Gallant off to the spacious loosebox rented for him. Being the richest girl in the district she felt she had the right to have her own way in everything.

Valerie's face was blank as she reached for her broom. It might not be riding, but there was always work in a stable yard to fill the days. It had to be enough.

Once Valerie had had her own pony, Calypso, and lived much the same life as Marina. But one day everything had come crashing down. Her parents had divorced and her father had gone off to America to a new life, full of promises to send them money to live on. His plane had crashed and so had their world; his debts had swallowed up the remaining capital. Trying to comfort her desolate mother in the bleak comfort of a tiny house with bulging walls which cracked the plaster and let in the damp, Valerie had had to contend, too, with her other tragic loss.

Calypso, a first class jumper, was up for sale when she rode him at that last show. Was she so upset that she had ridden carelessly? Had he felt her mood, as ponies do? He had put in a short stride at the parallel bars, taking off too late, dropping a leg between the bars and snapping it as he fell, leaving Valerie unconscious, also with a broken leg. Valerie had been taken to hospital where, after weeks of treatment, she had been nursed back to health, but there was nothing anyone could do for Calypso. He had been put down and dragged away to the knackers.

Her mother had thought that the shock of the loss would have put her daughter off ponies for good, but Valerie found them a consolation. There were so many problems she could not solve in her new life but looking after ponies made her feel that she could still do something. Even so, the mere idea of riding them made her muscles tighten up, her mouth quiver.

Valerie was so good in the stables, always ready to do any job, a marvel with a nervous pony, that she was worth her weight in gold. Miss Denison would have been more than glad to give her free rides for such competent help, better sometimes than her qualified assistant. It was ironic that the best helper she had did it for nothing, for the sheer pleasure of being near ponies.

As the children put the tack away, cars began to arrive. Their mothers grouped together to collect bunches of children on a weekly rota, until at last only Marina was left. In the terms of the livery she was supposed to 'do' her own pony on days she rode, but unless Miss Denison was actually watching she usually managed to slip out of it. She knew Valerie would never sneak on her, but would do the work herself rather than let Gallant be neglected.

The chauffer-driven black car glided into the yard and stopped beside Marina, who waved an airy hand at Valerie. "Finish off Gallant for me, will you?" she shouted. "I have to go to the station to meet Daddy." Valerie nodded, her face expressionless. Of all the ponies, Gallant was the most like Calypso, but she had never ridden Gallant, or wanted to ride him.

With Gallant settled comfortably, Valerie filled a bucket with two feeds; there was still one job to do on the way home. In a field at the top of the hill between the stables and the village were two driving ponies, enjoying a well-earned rest from scurry classes while their owner was abroad on holiday. Valerie fed them every morning and evening, on her way to and from Unicorn Stables, keeping sacks of feed at her home for the morning feeds. Fortunately a bubbling spring rose in their field, trickling down the hillside, so fresh water was always available.

Honker, the donkey, lived there permanently, but he did not mind company, viewing the various visitors with sad eyes as he chewed on a tuft of grass. He had been rescued, in a shocking state, from owners who had kept him in an outhouse and fed him on household scraps. He had been 'so sweet' when they had bought him as a fluffy foal, but their ignorance and ill-treatment had turned him into a wreck when he was still quite young.

Valerie was halfway up the hill, pink-faced and puffing, the heavy bucket of feed hanging from her handlebars, the bicycle feeling heavier with every step, when the big black car purred up beside her and stopped.

Marina leant out, waving wildly. "Have you heard the news?" she asked. "Daddy told me. Jake Larborough has bought the Orchard Stud property; he's moving all his showjumpers down here. He'll be right next door to us. Won't it be super? We'll actually *meet* him! Perhaps he'll let me..."

Marina's voice died away as her father ordered the chauffeur to drive on, too tired after his day in the City to listen to childish chatter, but the gleam in her eyes finished the sentence for her. It was obvious that she could already see herself exercising international showjumpers, being asked to school them...

"International showjumpers are always out on the circuit; we're not likely to see him very often," said Valerie but she said it to herself; the car had disappeared over the crest of the hill.

Reaching the gate, Valerie looked round in surprise; usually the two grey ponies, Seafoam and Spindrift, came rushing up to squabble over their feed, but this time there was no sign of them. Anxiously, Valerie checked that she had padlocked the chain on the gate, but it was still locked. Opening it, Valerie pushed the gate back and lifted the bucket off the bicycle, swinging it into the field and shutting the gate behind her.

"Seafoam, Spindrift!" shouted Valerie, looking round the steep field. A whinny answered her and suddenly the ponies charged into sight, ears back, snapping at each other, looking thoroughly cross. "Have you two been quarrelling?" asked Valerie, surprised.

The reason for the ponies' bad temper came walking across the field, beside Honker the donkey. He was a big chestnut, his shining coat rippling with muscle. The ponies stopped beside Valerie, unable to decide whether to chase off the stranger or to try to eat their feeds first. Lifting threatening heels at the chestnut's approach, they settled on the feeds.

Valerie tipped the feeds into two well-separated boxes – Seafoam was a terrible bully and would have chased off Sprindrift and eaten both shares, if he had had the chance – and walked towards Honker and his new friend, talking softly. There was always a handful of feed in the bottom of the bucket for the donkey, so that he didn't feel left out, though his lazy life in the paddock was already luxury beyond his wildest dreams.

This time, as soon as the donkey was munching, she offered the bucket to the chestnut, reaching out a hand to grasp the eighteen inches of broken rope dangling from the leather headcollar. The horse accepted her controlling hand almost gratefully, but Valerie wondered if she really was in control. Now that she had caught him, what could she do with him?

Leading him over to the gate, she waited until the ponies had finished their feeds. Seafoam rushed over to see if Sprindrift had left anything, but his partner was no fool; he always gobbled his food as fast as possible! Valerie decided that she had better lead the chestnut down to the stables where he could at least be stabled, while they tried to trace his owner. But the decision was taken out of her hands.

"Hey, what are you doing with that horse?" asked a man's voice. Surprised, Valerie turned round and saw a young man on horseback staring at her over the hedge. "I found him in the field when I came to feed the ponies," she replied. "I was just wondering what to do with him."

"It's lucky he's safe," said the young man. "Hold on a moment, I'm coming in." Backing a few paces he drove the horse forward into a neat jump over the hedge and reined in, perfectly in control.

Valerie was staring, open-mouthed. "You... you're Jake Larborough," she said. "You've bought the Orchard Stud."

"News always travels fast in the country," said Jake Larborough, grinning. "I was pretty sure someone would have seen Wonder. I was just worried that he might have gone down the hill to the main road. He's a perfect pest at home; he thinks he's an equine version of Houdini the escape artiste. He'd make a jolly good burglar – he can open anything!"

Valerie giggled. "He didn't open the padlocked gate," she said. "He must have jumped into the field, like you."

"Probably looking for company, once he'd lost himself. He ran away when Hetty, my head groom, was just taking off the last of his travelling bandages. Lunged back on the rope, snapped it and bolted. He's a funny horse – he loves being on the circuit, with all the excitement of shows, but he hates being at home. He never pulls these tricks when we're on the road."

"Golden Wonder! Of course," gasped Valerie. "I've often seen him on TV."

"Like horses, do you?" asked Jake. "You must come and see us at the new place. How about tomorrow, about this time? I'll introduce you to them, or Hetty will. Would you like that?"

Valerie nodded, too excited to speak. A faint look of alarm crossed Jake's face. "I do mean just looking. I can't afford amateurs on my horses. With the competition what it is, you have to know what you are doing on these horses; one stumble and a bit of heat in a leg can cost a fortune in prize money."

"I don't... I wouldn't dream of asking to ride your horses," stammered Valerie. "I just like helping to look after them down at Unicorn Stables."

"That's fine, then," said Jake. "We'll be here 'til the middle of next week, settling in. I've leased the place until the contracts are signed. It all takes time and I don't have any to waste. If you'll open the gate for me I'll lead Wonder back – I don't want to give him any more clever ideas about jumping hedges."

Valerie shooed the curious ponies back and put a restraining hand on Honker's nose as he moved closer to Wonder, obviously finding the showjumper's company more agreeable than that of Seafoam and Spindrift, who were usually inseparable, being so used to working in double harness.

Holding the gate wide, she watched Jake ride through and turn up the hill, the sound of eight hooves on the hard road drowned by the incessant complaints of Honker. It was the first time Valerie had ever heard the donkey express an opinion about anything. Usually he accepted life with stoical patience.

Pulling the gate shut, Valerie tightened the chain and clipped the padlock through the links before jumping on her bicycle; with an ecstatic sigh she pedalled off home. She had actually met and talked to Jake Larborough and he had invited her to see his horses. Marina would be furious. Valerie was giggling as she wheeled her bicycle into the lean-to beside the crumbling cottage. Watching from the window, Mrs. Jones smiled too; it was the first time she had seen Valerie look happy for a long time.

At Unicorn Stables the next day, Valerie had difficulty hiding her excitement, but she wanted to keep it a secret until she had really been to Orchard Stud. It was so difficult to believe that it had not all been a dream!

"Mummy is inviting Jake Larborough to a cocktail party next weekend," said Marina, importantly. "Everyone wants to meet him." She was too busy looking round for envious faces – 'everyone' did not include any of the Unicorn Stables riders – to notice Valerie's secret amusement. Jake would have left Orchard Stud to join the showjumping circuit by the end of the week, so the guest of honour would be missing!

It was a busy day at the stable, but everything seemed to be done in a trice. After feeding the two greys a little earlier than usual, Valerie was going to ride her bicycle through the massive gates and up the imposing drive to the showjumper's yard, to meet the horses she had only ever seen before on television.

Valerie's feet had wings as she climbed the steep hill to the waiting ponies and divided the feed. For once they would have to manage by themselves and if Spindrift didn't eat fast enough, he would have to defend himself. Looking round for Honker, to give him his handful, she saw him standing further up the field, craning into the hedge, long ears pricked forward. Opening his mouth, nostrils wide, he started to bray discordantly. Even when she called him, he did not turn his head.

Then Valerie heard it too; the sound of galloping hooves, thundering on the tarmac, a horse coming along the road. A moment later she saw Golden Wonder, galloping flat out, ears flattened into his mane, two boys on motor cycles behind him, whooping and shrieking, playing cowboys, driving the terrified horse ever faster. "Stop it!" screamed Valerie.

Scrambling over the gate as the horse passed her, she flung herself onto her bicycle and out onto the road. Not expecting this eruption from the gateway, the motor cyclists lost control, skidded on screaming tyres, slid and collided, crashing to the ground in a grinding screech of tearing metal.

Valerie did not even spare them a glance. At the bottom of the hill was the main road. If Golden Wonder didn't kill himself, he might kill someone else, crashing into a passing car. Ahead of her, at a bend in the road, the horse slipped and nearly fell. Recovering his balance he set off again, but more slowly this time, his nostrils scarlet, his eyes glazed with fear. But the terrifying pursuit had gone. The road evened out a little before it reached the main road.

Thankfully, Valerie saw that she was gaining on him; he was slowing down, as frightened of the roaring lorries on the main road as he had been of the motor cycles. A moment later Valerie drew alongside and reached out a hand for his headcollar, putting all her weight on it. A car turned into the road in front of her, making her gasp with fright, but the driver swerved across the road and stepped out to help her, advancing with outstretched arms. It was Jake.

"What on earth happened?" he asked. "What's the crazy horse done this time?" Valerie explained and Jake's face darkened. "I'll teach those brutes a lesson," he said furiously. "Just let me catch them!"

"I think they'll need an ambulance more than a lesson," said Valerie. "There was the most awful crash when I suddenly emerged from the gateway, but it did stop them chasing him. If he had kept going at that speed, all the way to the main road..." she shuddered. "I hope Wonder's alright; he nearly fell at the bend in the road."

"He looks alright," said Jake. "He's sound, anyway. I'll have to go and see what the damage is with the brutes. They'll be lucky if they've broken all their legs, otherwise I'll do it for them. Can you take Wonder home? His manners are perfect under saddle, you won't have any trouble. You can go across my land if you turn in at the next gate – but I expect you know your way around here better than I do. There's some tack and a hard hat in the back of the car."

Valerie turned red and then white. She felt sick and started to shake. Golden Wonder dropped his nose into her hand and snuffled gently, almost as if he was thanking for her saving his life. Valerie stood and watched speechlessly, her throat too choked to utter a sound, as Jake tacked him up and told her to put her bicycle down; he'd take it on to the stud for her.

He bent to give her a leg up. Mesmerised, Valerie let herself be thrown up into the saddle and picked up the reins. It all felt so natural that she wondered why she had not been on a horse for so long. Jake watched her keenly; this was, after all, his top showjumper. Loading the bicycle into his car, he parked it well into the side of the road, before walking with her to the gate, to let her onto his property. Wonder moved sedately, neck arched, playing with his bit.

"He must have wanted to see you again," said Jake, grinning.

Valerie shook her head. "I don't think he was looking for me; I think he was looking for Honker. They seemed to like each other yesterday. Perhaps, if you kept Honker with him, Wonder wouldn't stray so much."

"Who owns him? asked Jake. "I don't want to deprive any little girl, but I'd do anything to help Wonder."

"No one can ride him," said Valerie. "He was rescued from an awful home by the lady who owns the greys, but they are a real pair, because she drives them in scurry competitions, so they don't take much notice of Honker. He has a bad leg – in fact, he has four bad legs – so he can't be ridden. I don't think she'd mind you having him, because she'd know that he'd be well treated and he does seem to like Wonder. He heard him coming long before I did."

Jake gave Valerie a long look. "You're quite a girl," he said. "There you are, on my best horse and I don't even know your name. If you'll take Wonder home for me, we'll have a long chat. Will your parents be worried? You can phone from the office Hetty has fixed up in the tack room."

"I only have a mother now," said Valerie, but for the first time it almost seemed enough. Perhaps she could make herself a life in the new world she had found so difficult to accept. "My name's Valerie Jones."

Jake opened the gate for her and said, "You go on to the yard and I'll go and inspect the scene of the accident. I may be a while if I have to call an ambulance, so phone your mother and tell her where you are.

"I want to talk to you about the future, if you want a career with horses. A girl who acts like that in an emergency is the sort of person I like to employ, if you are interested when you leave school. There'll be a heap of exams to pass to get you qualified, but there's plenty of opportunity to gain experience around my yard." Waving his hand, he shut the gate on her and walked back to his car.

Valerie's mind was running wild, imagining, dreaming, thinking... but then she came down to earth. She was riding a valuable horse and he deserved all her attention. She rode along the track by the hedge at a collected walk, not wanting to take any risks. She had quite forgotten that the field bordered the property where Marina Barker lived – she and her mother had never been invited to the Barker parties.

A window shot up as she passed the house and she saw Marina's astonished face. "What are you doing, Valerie?" shouted Marina. "That's the Orchard Stud land. Who is that horse? Why are you riding him?"

"He's Jake Larborough's top showjumper," said Valerie. "I'm just taking him home for Jake."

Riding on, with Wonder waving an astonished ear at her giggles, Valerie listened to the screaming stream of questions following her across the field, but she had other things to think about now.

For the first time since her father's death and Calypso's dreadful fall she was not running away from life, from living in the only way she really wanted. Perhaps, with Honker as a companion, Golden Wonder would stop running away, too.

★ ★ ★

illustration by Steve Humfress

GOOD PROSPECTS

By Rosemary Simmonds

I was determined to get a job working with horses, despite Mum and Dad's protestations. But after working all hours for a pittance I finally accepted that there were other ways to make a career out of my horsy obsession.

"I am going," I said determinedly, my jaw set, my hands tight with defiance.

My mother sat down and ran her fingers through her hair. "Lonsdale is in the middle of nowhere. What if you need a dentist or you are ill?"

"There are such things as buses. Anyway, Mrs Baydon would take me, people help each other in the country."

She shook her head hopelessly. "You should go to college and get yourself trained for a proper job."

"This is a proper job! I'll be paid. You should be glad I've taken the initiative. Isn't that what everyone complains about these days? Young people want everything handed to them on a plate."

"Just how much will you be paid?" Dad asked quietly.

My stomach crinkled and I wished I had not mentioned money in front of him. However much I was being paid would seem a pittance compared to his salary. "Twenty pounds a week," I admitted.

"Slave labour," Mum wailed.

"It isn't. I'm lucky to be paid at all considering I've no experience and I'll be trained on the job. Besides I'm getting free bed and board and I'll be with horses all day long – that's all I want!"

I flung out of the room but Dad's voice trailed after me with cutting sarcasm. "Just as well because that's all you'll be getting. It costs a lot more to stay alive in this world than twenty pounds."

I shut my ears to him. I wanted to work with horses and by God I was going to.

No way was I going to stay in the house for the rest of the afternoon. I got my bicyle out and took off for Heaton Hill Stables to find Louise. *She* would appreciate how lucky I was.

Heaton Hill was as spotless as ever. I had learned to ride there and once past my sixteenth birthday Mrs Ricketts, unaffectionately known as 'The Colonel', pemitted me to help out at weekends. That's how I came to meet Louise. She had a half-Thoroughbred called Escapade liveried there. If I'd sweet-talked Mrs Ricketts she might have given me a job but it would mean obeying her strict orders, wearing a uniform of navy jodhpurs and sweatshirt and brushing the yard every five minutes.

Louise was in the stable, saddling up. "That's great," she said when I told her about the job. She did not seem very enthusiastic though.

"Is something wrong?" I asked.

"Sorry, I'm a bit out of sorts. Someone is coming to try out Escapade. I know I have to sell him but it still hurts."

"You'll feel better when you get Sprite over to replace him."

"Yes. Hey, write me lots of letters to brighten my boring days at Durrows."

"I thought you liked it there."

"No fear. I might as well never have sweated to learn shorthand – all I do is file and make tea. I'm already looking for a better job."

Boredom was something I'd never have to contend with in the job I had chosen.

I hugged my cases to me as the bus dropped me off at the edge of Londsale village. Almost there. . . '*almost*' turned out to be another two miles and my suitcases grew heavier with each stride.

At last the sign came into view. The lane was concreted for twenty yards where it turned sharp right to a modern bungalow. The door was opened by a small woman in stone-washed jeans and a loose Snoopy sweatshirt.

"Mrs Boyden?" I stammered.

"Call me Shirley. You must be Karen."

I nodded, struck dumb by the difference between her and The Colonel.

"I'll show you the caravan, then we'll go and feed the horses. You don't mind starting right away, do you?" She kicked off moccasin slippers and pushed her feet into thick socks and wellingtons, then led me along the potholed lane to the stableyard.

Three modern timber boxes gave onto concrete, so old it had turned into crazy paving. Thoroughbred heads, a bay and a grey, popped over the doors. The bay whinnied in welcome – or was it for food? "Gay Abandon is my point-to-pointer," said Shirley. "The grey, Fair Trial, is my friend's event horse."

I nodded, my mouth watering as I imagined exercising these noble creatures.

Next to the boxes was a barn containing a dozen bales of hay and straw and two hurdle pens. In the cubbyhole between these two buildings my tiny caravan lodged. The third edge of the yard was taken up by one of those corrugated byre affairs that look like a split cucumber. Inside were a dozen pig pens that would make stalls for small ponies, a tack depot and feed bins. The office was a breeze-block building tacked on the end.

There were eleven animals in all; the two Thoroughbreds; a cobby bay who led most of the rides; a nervous fifteen hand chestnut mare with Arab blood. Then there were the ponies, starting with a fourteen-hand black gelding, Archie, and working down through Revel, Echo, Snowy, Toffo and Tawny to a brown Shetland called Pickle who was lethal with his back feet.

The first days were hectic but I soon settled into a pattern of work. My alarm shrilled me from happy sleep at six-thirty to feed the animals and bring the ponies in from the field.

After my own breakfast I groomed the ponies that would be used for the first ride at eleven and helped the children to tack up and mount. While they were out I groomed the rest of the ponies, then snatched a quick lunch at the bungalow when Mrs Boyden came back. Another ride went out at two, which was my time for mucking out. After that there was a round of feeding, turning out and tack cleaning.

Shirley sometimes took the Arab mare out in the late afternoon. It didn't take long to see why she was never used for rides. They had a battle every time they approached the lane and it took a hefty whack from Shirley's leather-covered crop to get the chestnut on her way. I had hoped I might get to ride her. That didn't seem likely now. In fact I was beginning to wonder if I would ever get on any of the ponies. I'd been here two weeks and had not been in the saddle once.

I had a halfday on Wednesday, but that was taken up by going into Lonsdale to do my laundry and pick up supplies. It didn't take long to learn that my father was right about the speed with which money could vanish, especially when I punctured my wellingtons and had to fork out for a new pair.

By the end of the first month I had managed to make friends with some of the children who came for rides and felt less lonely.

Angela Taite, a twelve-year-old girl from the village, often stayed behind after her ride to help out, even rolling back her sleeves to embark on the tack room.

Angela was at the stables grooming Revel and Echo on the afternoon Shirley returned to the yard at full gallop. Cherish put in a skid stop then started dancing about. "Turn her out for me, Karen," Shirley said, jumping down. She headed for the bungalow pretty smartish but not before Angela and I had seen the long muddy patch on her denim jodhpurs. "You naughty girl," I admonished Cherish, but she was too full of herself to listen.

Shirley did not ride again that afternoon. She was going shopping, she told me. I was to take the afternoon ride. "I've been meaning to give you a horse to work on yourself," she added. "See what you can do with Cherish." I greeted the offer with diminished enthusiasm; the ground was hard to fall on.

I shifted my jobs around a bit the following day to give me time to ride Cherish. Nerves made my stomach jitter but I was determined to go ahead. I wished I had a teacher on hand to help, but Shirley had done one of her famous vanishing tricks and left me to my own devices.

Cherish sidled away from me when I turned the stirrup to mount. "Now then," I coaxed, "you be good with me." Her ears flicked back and she scowled dreadfully. Rather than drag back on the reins as I had seen Shirley do, I decided to leave her fairly loose and took one hand from the rein to stroke her silky neck.

Gradually the stiffness went out of her shoulders and I sprang lightly into the saddle. Cherish started walking backwards. I put my hands forward to slacken the rein and closed my legs to her ribs as The Colonel had told us to do. Cherish brought her head up, her ears pricked and she walked on. She remained very jumpy but she did go forward and I made sure my reins were so soft she had nothing to pit herself against.

I took to riding Cherish whenever I had the time. It gave me a special kind of thrill to feel her responding to me and to know by the easy way she took up the bit that she was looking forward to her ride.

Louise wrote long letters about Sprite and I wrote back carefully edited ones about life at the stables. Come October she wrote to say she was entering a one day event at Langthwaite, not far away, and would I come to cheer her on.

I asked Shirley after work.

"You can't be serious, Karen, you know how busy we are at weekends."

"But I haven't had a full day off since I came."

"Your day off must be taken midweek, you know that."

"I'll have next Tuesday off then," I snapped and marched to the barn where Cherish put her head over the fence to nuzzle me. "We'll go out all day on Tuesday," I said, stroking her nose. "Right up onto the moor, just you and me."

Feeling sorry for myself, I hijacked the office phone and dialled Louise's number.

"She's worse than The Colonel!" Louise exclaimed after hearing my tale.

"She does have a point. We take four rides on Saturdays."

"I suppose so. Hey, guess who's got a new job!"

"Where?"

"Evening Gazette. Selling classified advertising. Don't laugh; the pay is twice what I was getting at Durrows. A hundred and thirty a week gross, not bad eh?"

"Let me know when you buy Sprite a diamond-studded bridle," I quipped but inwardly I cringed. No wonder Dad had seen red when I boasted about my wages.

Louise laughed. "I'm saving up to take Sprite for a week's intensive training in Harrogate – you'll see me at Badminton yet!"

I put the receiver down. My limbs felt as limp as chewed string. Louise might not live amongst horses as I did but her riding was improving ten times as quickly. I cleaned the tack with minimum effort and headed for soup and cheese in my caravan, turning the volume dial on my cassette player to the top of the scale in an effort to cheer myself up. Cold drizzle pressed against the windows.

I put off making a last round of the stables until half-nine, then dashed out with a torch, checking the byre and office doors were padlocked and letting the Thoroughbreds into their stables out of the rain. The ponies were huddled under a big sycamore for shelter: all except Cherish.

Seconds later I was tying the broken fence with baler twine, thankful the other ponies had been too busy sheltering to follow the mare's escape. Then off I went with the mud sucking at my boots, following Cherish's hoofprints by the light of my feeble torch. I seemed to tramp for hours around fields and down unknown lanes. The drizzle turned to pounding rain that seeped through the shoulder seams of my coat and made my jeans stick clammily to my thighs.

Cherish saw me first. She put up her head and whickered in such a friendly way you'd never believe she had been so naughty. I looked at the big white house behind the cedars and the deep holes Cherish had made in their bowling-green lawn and prayed no one had seen her. Thankfully she let me catch her easily; perhaps the adventure had worn off with the rain. Back we went as water found a way into my boots.

Lights flashed on the wet road. I pushed Cherish onto the verge. The car overtook then braked. Shirley Boyden's head poked out.

"Karen?"

I pulled Cherish closer. "She got out of the field," I explained, leaning down to the open window. "She's alright."

"Carry on then," Shirley said merrily and drove away, leaving behind her the scent of brandy.

During the long walk back I could not avoid facing the truth. I might stay here for a hundred years and I'd still be mucking out for twenty pounds a week and a leaky caravan.

The phrase 'a job with prospects' suddenly made blinding sense. But what else could I do? If I went home my parents would have me behind the counter at the Westminster before I knew what had hit me. I'd just have to soldier on. Next time I went into town I would buy a copy of 'Horse and Hound' and start looking for another job. The decision sounded brave in my head but my stomach quivered and I felt dreadfully alone.

The next morning I woke feeling as though someone had laced my eyelids with lead and filled my head with concrete while I slept. The horses were neighing for breakfast, making my head ring with their din. "I'm coming," I muttered, dragging on my jeans.

Shirley appeared beneath dark glasses for just long enough to tell me to take the morning ride. My lips tightened as I muttered something unmentionable in reply.

I took the ride through the woods, walking all the time. My head throbbed dully and sweat made my shirt stick to my back. I seemed to be looking at the world through a long tunnel. Then it all went black.

The next thing I knew I was lying on a settee in front of a roaring fire. I turned my head slowly. Muffled voices came from beyond the door. A man said, "She'll be alright once she comes round but she is running a frightful temperature. Nasty dose of 'flu."

A woman said, "We are taking her home."

"That would be best," the doctor agreed.

The door opened and my mother came in. "Karen, you are awake! How do you feel?"

"Okay." Actually I had a raging throat and my side ached. "What happened?"

"You fainted. And now, young lady, no arguments – you are coming home with us."

"But the horses..."

"They'll have to manage without you. Your father has gone to get your things."

I tried to argue but didn't have the strength.

Once I had recovered my parents brought up the subject of my future once again. There was the usual pep talk about prospects and security. But they ended up by saying that as I had proved I was determined and not afraid of hard work they would support my wish to work with horses – if I went through proper training.

Dad dropped a sheaf of leaflets in my lap. "Louise sent us these," he said. They showed a brick college with its own stable block. Classroom lessons were photographed against instruction in a sawdust ring. Bold lettering pointed out that the college offered riding and stable management instruction with affiliated studies; business, secretarial or cookery skills.

"All the big stables need office staff as well," Mum pointed out. "A course like that would make you more versatile, you would have more skills to sell."

I nodded. They were right. Not that I hankered after a stuffy office job but I didn't want a dead end one in the horse world either. Those months at Lonsdale had taught me to follow Louise's lead – if I wanted to get satisfaction out of my career it would be up to me to make something of it!

Two months later I came back from college to hear Mum calling me to the telephone.

"Hello, it's Angela. Mrs Boyden is closing down, too much effort to keep it running in the winter and she couldn't get anyone else to help full-time. She's keeping the big horses and buying a couple of brood mares in. The ponies are all up for sale. I thought you might like Cherish."

My seventeenth birthday was coming up but I was sure the chestnut would be expensive. "I'll never afford her," I told Angela sadly.

"You will, she's been bucking people off ever since you left. No one round here will touch her."

I smiled. Cherish, what a madam she was! "I'll see what I can do and phone you back."

Would Mum and Dad agree to lend me the money to buy the mare, I wondered?

To my surprise and delight they offered to buy her for my birthday present.

So Cherish came to college too – and bucked me off a couple of times before she learned her manners again I might add!

illustration by Claire Colvin

EMMA

By Catherine Maclean

Ragtime and I were at a show when I first met Emma. She was so friendly you could not be jealous of her brilliant riding and beautiful horse. No one could have foreseen the tragedy that would befall them...

This isn't a 'red rosette at the gymkhana and happy ever after' kind of story, but it's not all bad and I think it's certainly worth knowing. It's made me think how lucky I am: how lucky most people are every hour and every minute. Our luck hangs by a thread that could snap any second, regardless of who we are and how charmed we appear. I hope that's how you'll feel too when you reach the end of this story.

Now that you're dying of suspense, I'd better tell you a little more about myself. My name's Tessa Hardcastle and I'm seventeen, but I was fifteen when I met Emma. I had a horse called Ragtime.

We bought him for my fifteenth birthday. I'd always dreamed of having a horse but never quite believed I really would. I'd ridden for years and had a couple of ponies on loan. It was a dream come true when Mum got promoted and we could actually afford a horse. I was walking on three feet of air, lost in a world of lungeing, schooling and local gymkhanas.

A few weeks later, exactly the right horse turned up on loan to the stables where I rode. He was there to find a 'suitable' owner. I fell in love with him the moment I saw him poking his nose over the field gate, looking cheekily at me through long black eyelashes.

I wasn't very good at riding him at first. He wasn't very schooled and supple but he was still an awful lot more responsive than the Fell pony I'd been riding for the previous few months. Ragtime and I tended to progress round the school in a series of jerky rushes and stops, watched by Jenny our cringeing instructor. We persevered and after a couple of months Jenny could watch without flinching as we did basic schooling and popped over a few cavaletti.

Best of all, Ragtime started to know me. When I walked across the field to get him, his head would go up, and if he were feeling especially frisky he would trot over to me, shaking his head, and nudge me playfully as if to say, "Come on, I'm here, give me a carrot and then let's get going"!

I was very nervous about the vetting. Partly because I would have to ride in front of the vet, Jenny, my parents and Mrs. Blakie, but mainly in case Ragtime had some horrible, incurable disease.

As it turned out, the vetting was really interesting and nothing awful came to light. The vet checked him over. The funniest bit was where Ragtime had his legs picked up and stretched out to see that his bones and joints were OK; the expression on his face was so long-suffering! Then I had to ride him at various paces in the school and lastly give him a brisk gallop up the field so the vet could check his heart and lungs.

At the end, the vet filled out his details on a form and let me see it: *'15hh bright bay TB/Welsh cob gelding, seven years old. Distinguishing marks – white star, white offhind foot, scar two inches long on near fore caused by barbed wire'.*

I stood and looked at the form and thought; "This horse is going to be *mine*." I kept saying it over and over in my head but it wouldn't sink in. The vet took back the form, put it in her case, snapped it shut and said brightly "Well, good luck, he seems a very nice gelding," and strode off to her car.

I stood in a daze, smiling goofily at Ragtime while my Dad and Mrs. Blakie discussed how much extra we should pay for his tack and New Zealand. My very own horse!

By May Jenny and I thought we were ready for 'the first show'. It was, more or less, a complete disaster. It was raining and cold, and I felt sick to the bottom of my stomach with nerves. Ragtime sensed that, and got totally over-excited, virtually destroying the clear round course. After that I withdrew from the showjumping, it looked so skyscrapingly huge.

I went through that show in such a haze of fear that I didn't even notice Emma Maxwell and Bittersweet cleaning up – they won every class in their age group. I found out later that Emma had noticed me.

The next couple of shows were marginally better and I began to take note of this girl that everyone talked about. Destined for the top, a blonde goddess on a beautiful iron grey mare with a silvery mane and tail. I watched enviously as they jumped clears at a collected, flowing pace.

Then, at my fourth show, Emma came up to chat to me, saying, "Hi – I've seen you at a few shows recently. Is he your own horse? He's lovely, looks a bit green though."

That's the kind of girl Emma Maxwell *was* . . .is . . . *was*. She was so friendly you couldn't hate her for her brilliance.

You might have noticed that an awful lot of people have undeserved success in the horse world, and a lot of people have undeserved failure. Everywhere you go there are parents who buy their kids push-button ponies. These perfect horses do everything brilliantly for a while; then, when they're ruined by their riders they are sold on and replaced by another model of expensive equine perfection. Other people who can ride just as well are stuck with Patch from the local riding school.

I'm in the middle – an OK rider on an OK horse. I would do better if I were competitive and ambitious, but I haven't got any killer instinct – I don't like to risk my neck or my horse's. To win you have to take risks.

Emma had it all. She was a great rider, really talented, and could probably have got a clear round out of a mule. She also had supportive and incredibly rich parents. For all her blonde prettiness, she was as tough as an old boot – killer instinct personified.

As she went round cross-country courses, she thought about risks and took them in split seconds, whereas I tend to slow up thinking, "That water jump looks awfully slippy. What if Ragtime falls and hurts himself?"

Emma was just as tough out hunting, jumping all the big fences and galloping for miles. It was something we always argued about because I don't hunt – I see no pleasure in a sport that involves chasing another animal and ripping it to bits. Emma couldn't imagine *not* hunting . . . and then the fox? Well, tough luck if it got caught – survival of the fittest and all that, you know.

Emma had a very strong will and imposed it on both horses and people. I suppose in a way she was spoilt, but she never had sulks or tantrums, and though she was very demanding she never pushed Bittersweet too far or punished her too much.

Of course, there were plenty of shows where Emma and Bittersweet *didn't* win everything. They had their share of falls and injuries, but in the time I knew them, they were always placed in at least one class at each show. The word was that they were ready to go places.

Bittersweet was fifteen-and-a-half hands, seven years old and a perfect match for Emma. They made a great team, combining ability, looks and a will to win. Bittersweet loved Emma as much as Ragtime was beginning to love me. Perhaps Emma didn't care quite as much for Bittersweet as I do for Ragtime; a good competing horse was more important to her than a nice character. In Bittersweet she had both. For all her affectionate, soppy nature in the stable, Bittersweet was as hard as nails out hunting, in a jump-off or on a cross-country course. She was hell-bent on doing it best and would have gone on 'til she dropped.

I went to Emma's house a few times and came back dazed! Imagine having your own all-weather surface arena and set of jumps. Bittersweet was kept beautifully, with Emma's tiny bad-tempered first pony as company. Unlike Pickles, on whom Emma had learned to ride at the age of five, Bittersweet had lovely manners.

Even the tack room looked as though it had come straight out of a story book – rosettes all over the walls, trophies, photos of Emma, Bittersweet and Emma's four previous ponies.

One sunny autumn day Emma mentioned casually that she'd qualified for a really big local one day event. Would I like to go with her and act as groom? Of course, I jumped at the chance. As the great day approached I seemed much more excited than Emma, although I think she was really pretty nervous, just covering it up well.

Bittersweet was in fantastic condition – coat clipped and shiny. After visiting the Maxwell's I'd stared ruefully at Ragtime's muddy, teddy-bearish appearance before feeding him some carrots. I used to promise him that one day I'd have enough money to keep him looking as smart as Bittersweet.

The day of the show was forecast cold, clear and sunny – just what we'd been hoping for. Getting up at five o'clock on a cold November morning to prepare for a show is hardly a bundle of laughs. We were both really tired because I'd stayed over at the Maxwell's and Emma had talked far into the night about her hopes for the future. I don't think I'd realised up 'til then quite how ambitious she was.

By the time we were pulling out onto the main road, with a plaited and bandaged Bittersweet in the back of the Maxwell's smart cream-coloured trailer, the weather was clear and sunny, much to our relief. It was nearly an hour's drive to the ground, and by the time we got there Emma was silent and white-faced, with her jaw set. I took off Bittersweet's bandages and rugs and put on her boots and tack while Emma changed in the trailer. She was wearing new white jodhpurs, black jacket and boots, and a white stock. Bittersweet and she made a fantastic pair; I was glad I'd remembered my camera in the last minute rush.

Emma warmed up and calmed Bittersweet, while I wandered round the grounds, staring in admiration at a few famous faces and in horror at the sheer size of the jumps.

I couldn't bear to watch Emma in the dressage so I walked the cross-country course. The ground was a little muddy, but it would not ride too badly as long as the dry weather kept up. Some of the jumps gave me the shudders – the water looked tricky and the coffin terrifying. I don't know how anyone could have been so twisted to think up a combination consisting of a jump, a steep downhill, a ditch, a steep uphill and another jump, and then to top it all by calling it a coffin!

I got back to find Emma declaring her dressage was "mediocre", but her parents looked quite pleased. There was quite a lot of hanging around before the showjumping and by the time she was warming up again the sky had clouded over. I stayed to watch this time as I wanted to take some photos.

Emma went into the ring too determined to win. I think it was this that made Bittersweet clip two jumps with her forefeet – eight faults. Emma was furious with herself but only said, "Well, I'll just have to try harder in the cross-country". We had some lunch and Emma changed into her silks.

The rain started so gradually we didn't notice it, but by the time we'd finished eating it was hammering down. People and horses huddled miserably under trees and there were notably fewer spectators. The announcer commented over the loudspeaker that there was quite a quagmire in front of certain jumps.

With four riders to go before her, Emma got on Bittersweet again. She didn't want to spend too long warming up as the mare disliked the rain. It had eased off a bit but was still heavy enough to make her flatten her ears and hunch her back miserably.

She brightened up when she saw the jumps and went over the first few in fine form. I walked to another part of the course and saw the pair again. Emma was crouched low over Bittersweet's neck and both were concentrating intensely as they swept by the next jump, oblivious of the rain and remaining spectators.

I was walking back to the trailer when the loudspeaker crackled into action, the commentator gabbling wildly:

"And – oh no – it's Emma Maxwell, number 74, she's down . . . her horse has fallen going into the coffin and – oh dear – this looks very serious – the ambulance is on its way . . ."

Every word up 'til that point is burned into my memory. I still have dreams where I'm standing there, frozen with terror, rain sliding down my neck in icy drops, and those words crackling out over and over again.

At the mention of the ambulance I stopped listening and then I was running wildly, slipping and sobbing for breath, in the direction of the coffin.

Once I could see the white splash of the ambulance in the distance, I stopped. People rushed by on either side of me, like vultures hungry to see the kill. I can't, I thought, I can't go any further. I tried desperately to block out the vision of my friend and her beautiful horse . . .

I was only able to move when it was announced that Bittersweet had been put down and the ambulancemen were trying to get Emma out of the coffin and onto a stretcher. I started to run again, crying as I went and concentrating on the stitch in my side in an effort not to think too much about Bittersweet . . . But Emma, Emma was alive . . . I clung desperately to the hope that she wasn't too badly hurt.

She was in a coma for a fortnight. I couldn't cry, couldn't face up to the possibility that she might not recover, I just knew she wouldn't die – I felt sure her iron will would pull her through.

It's a year and half later and it seems as clear as yesterday, although in a far-off kind of way, like looking down the wrong end of a telescope. I still don't know why Bittersweet was put down. I could find out if I asked but I don't want to know.

And Emma? Emma's quite happy, living at home with her parents.

Although she is 17, like me, she has a mental age of six and will never grow past that.

I still see her a lot. She attends a special school for the mentally handicapped and twice a week goes to a Riding for the Disabled stables. I go too, and lead Major, the 19-year-old cob she rides. She had to learn to ride again from scratch, but she's pretty good.

You may have noticed that throughout this story I've generally referred to Emma in the past tense. That's because Emma before the accident and Emma after it are very divided in my mind. Really the accident hasn't altered her that much – she's still friendly, pretty and made of steely determination. She told me last week that one day she means to be a champion disabled rider, the best in Britain – if not the world. Some things never change.

Though there are days when the loss of what might have been, the pain and the suffering seem unbearable, most of the time I feel it's not *too* bad. Emma is happy. She doesn't remember Bittersweet, she doesn't know she used to be a brilliant young rider heading for the international showjumping circuit. She loves her school and most of all she loves Major. She's made a lot of new friends and still counts me as one of her best.

And me? I've still got Ragtime. We've both come on beautifully, but I'll never be able to jump a coffin again . . .